About the author

Alexander Solzhenitsyn was born into a middle class family at Rostov-on-Don in 1918. After graduating from Rostov University, he began his military service and gradually worked his way up to the rank of captain. Early in 1945 Solzhenitsyn was arrested and charged with making insulting remarks about Stalin. The punishment for this crime was eight years' confinement in forced labour camps – first with common criminals in the Arctic, and later in special camps for long term prisoners, including the camp at Karraganda which inspired *One Day in the Life of Ivan Denisovich*. After Stalin's death in 1953 Solzhenitsyn was eventually released. *One Day in the Life of Ivan Denisovich* was submitted to Tvardovsky, poet and editor of the literary journal *Novy Mir*, in 1960; two years later the text of the novel was included in the eleventh issue of the journal, which sold out at once. Solzhenitsyn's exposure of the concentration camp system and his scathing indictment of Soviet bureaucracy attracted the attention of the authorities and steps were taken to prevent the publication of other works by the author. When *The First Circle* and *Cancer Ward* were circulated in manuscript form, he was openly condemned by the establishment press and has since had to face endless harassment and persecution. But while hostility towards Solzhenitsyn has grown inside Russia, his outstanding literary merits have been recognised outside his own country, and his efforts to secure creative freedom for Soviet writers have been widely admired. Solzhenitsyn was awarded the 1970 Nobel Prize for Literature.

*Also by Alexander Solzhenitsyn
and available from Sphere Books*

FOR THE GOOD OF THE CAUSE
WE NEVER MAKE MISTAKES
and a Sphere Special Screenplay of
ONE DAY IN THE LIFE OF IVAN DENISOVICH

One Day in the Life of Ivan Denisovich

ALEXANDER SOLZHENITSYN

Translated by Gillon Aitken

SPHERE BOOKS LIMITED
30/32 Gray's Inn Road, London WC1X 8JL

First published in Great Britain by
Sphere Books Ltd. 1970
Copyright © W-Leontes-Norskfilm 1970
Reprinted February 1971, April 1971, January 1974

Set in Monotype Times New Roman

Printed in Great Britain by
C. Nicholls & Company Ltd.
The Philips Park Press, Manchester

ISBN 0 7221 8026 8

ONE DAY IN THE LIFE OF
IVAN DENISOVICH

At 5.00 a.m., as usual, reveille was sounded – a hammer banged against a rail just by the staff barracks. The intermittent ringing came faintly through the window-panes, two fingers thick with frost, and died away rapidly: it was cold, and the warder did not want to go on banging for long.

The noise stopped, and outside the window it was pitch dark when Shukhov got up to go to the latrines; it was as dark as night. Then the yellow light from three lamps – two on the perimeter; one inside the camp – fell on the window.

For some reason nobody had come to open up the barracks; and there was no sound of the orderlies lifting up a latrine barrel onto poles in order to carry it away.

Shukhov never overslept reveille, but always got up at once – which gave him, until parade, about ninety minutes to himself, unordained, and anyone who knew camp life could always earn himself something – by sewing someone a cover for his mittens out of a piece of old lining; by fetching some affluent gang-leader his dry felt boots – right up to his bunk so that the fellow would not have to stumble about barefoot around the pile looking for his own; or by going around to the store-rooms where someone might be able to use him, sweeping or carrying something; by going to the mess-hall to pick up the bowls from the tables and take them in piles to the dish-washer – there was always a chance of getting something to eat, although there were too many others with the same idea – and, what's worse, if you found something left in a bowl, you couldn't resist starting to lick it out. And Shukhov had never forgotten the words of his first gang-leader, Kuzyomin – an old lag who had already been inside for twelve

7

years in 1943 – who told some new arrivals from the front as they sat by a bonfire in a barren forest clearing:

"Here, lads, it's the law of the jungle. But even here people can live. The first to go under is the fellow who licks out bowls, who puts his trust in the infirmary, or who squeals on his mates."

He wasn't so right about the squealers, they could get by all right – only at the expense of other people's blood.

Shukhov always got up at reveille, but today he didn't. He had been feeling rotten since the previous evening, feverish and with pains all over his body. He had not been able to keep warm through the night. In his sleep he had felt that he was becoming really ill at one moment, at another that he was improving. He had dreaded the morning.

But the morning came as it always did.

Anyway, how could he have got warm – the ice thick on the window, and a white cobweb of frost all along the barracks where the walls joined the ceiling.

Shukhov did not get up. He lay on his top bunk, his head covered by a blanket and coat, his feet tucked into the sleeves – folded back at the ends – of his jacket. He could not see, but he understood by the noises around, what was going on in the barracks and in the corner occupied by his gang. There, the heavy tread along the corridor of the orderlies carrying one of the latrine barrels. This was considered light work, a job for a sick man, but to carry the thing without spilling it! Then some men from Gang 75 slammed a pile of felt boots from the drying-room on the floor. Then some men from his own gang did the same (today it was the turn of his gang to dry their felt boots). The gang-leader and his second-in-command quietly put on their boots, although their bunks creaked as they did so. The second-in-command would now go out to the bread-store – the leader to the Production Planning Department (PPD) at the staff barracks.

But Shukhov remembered that this would not simply

be a routine trip to the PPD for orders. Today was a fateful day: they wanted to transfer their gang – 104 – from the construction of workshops to a new project, the "Socialist Community Centre". The Centre was simply a barren field covered with snow-drifts, and before anything could be done there, they would have to dig holes, erect posts and put up barbed wire between the posts – to prevent themselves from escaping. And only then could they begin to build.

You could be sure that there would be nowhere to get warm for a month – not even a dog-hole. And it would be impossible to have a fire – where to get the fuel? The only hope would be to keep warm through work.

The gang-leader was anxious, would have to try to arrange matters – to push some other gang, less alert, into the job. Of course, he wouldn't get anywhere if he went empty-handed. It would mean a pound of lard to the senior official, perhaps two.

There's no harm in trying, why not go up to the infirmary and aim for a few days off work? Anyway, his whole body ached.

Then – which warder was on duty today?

He remembered – "One-and-a-half" Ivan, a tall, gaunt, black-eyed sergeant. The first time you saw him, you thought what a terror – but when you got to know him, he was the most lenient of all the warders – wouldn't slap you in the cells, wouldn't drag you up before the chief disciplinary officer. So it was all right to stay in his bunk for a while – until Barracks 9 had to go to the mess-hall.

The bunk began to rock and shake. Two of his neighbours started to get up at the same time – parallel to him, the Baptist Alyoshka, and below, the ex-naval captain Buinovsky.

Having carried out both the latrine barrels, two elderly orderlies began to quarrel as to who should go for the hot water. They nagged away at each other like a

9

couple of old women. The electric welder in Gang 20 roared at them:

"Hey, you splutterers" – and he flung a boot at them – "I'll shut you up!"

The boot thudded against a post. The orderlies shut up.

The second-in-command of the gang next to them growled softly:

"Vasily Fyodorovitch! They've cheated us at the supply-store, the swine: we should have four 900-gram loaves, and we've only got three. Who's going to go short?"

He spoke quietly, but, of course, everybody in the gang heard him and held his breath: who would get less bread than he should this evening?

Shukhov continued to lie on the hard-packed sawdust of his mattress. If only it could be one thing or another – either a real fever or an end to the pain. It was neither the one nor the other.

While the Baptist was whispering his prayers, Buinovsky returned from the latrines and announced to nobody in particular, but with a kind of glee:

"Well, men, buck up then! It's thirty below without doubt."

Shukhov decided to go to the infirmary.

And then some powerful hand stripped his jacket and blanket off him. Shukhov snatched his coat from his face and began to sit up. Below him, his head level with the top of the bunk, stood the spare figure of "The Tartar".

So he had come on duty out of turn and stolen up on them.

"S–854," The Tartar read from the white strip sewn to the back of Shukhov's black coat, "three days' in the cells with work!"

As soon as his unusual, constrained voice was heard, everyone not already up in the whole half-dark barracks, where not all the lights were on and where two

10

hundred men slept in fifty bug-ridden bunks, immediately came to life and began rapidly to get dressed.

"But why, Comrade Warder?" asked Shukhov in a voice expressive of greater self-pity than he felt.

"With work" – it could have been twice as bad. They gave you hot food, and you didn't have time to start thinking. The cells without work – that was the full treatment.

"For not getting up at reveille. Come with me to the Commandant's office," The Tartar explained indifferently – because he, and Shukhov, and everybody else understood perfectly well what the punishment was for.

There was no expression on The Tartar's hairless, crumpled face. He turned, looking for another victim, but everybody, in the darker parts of the barracks and under the lights, on the lower bunks and on the higher, was pushing his legs into the black, padded trousers with numbers on the left knee, or, already dressed, was wrapping himself up and hastening outside – to avoid The Tartar until he left.

If Shukhov had been punished for something he deserved, he would not have been so pained. What upset him was that he was always one of the first to get up. But he knew it was impossible to plead with The Tartar. And, while continuing to remonstrate for form's sake, Shukhov at the same time pulled on his padded trousers (which also had a worn, bedraggled scrap of cloth sewn above the left knee, with the number S–854 painted on it in black and already faded), put on his jacket (which had two numbers on it – one on the front and one on the back), and went out after The Tartar.

The whole of Gang 104 saw Shukhov go, but nobody said a word: what would have been the use, and what could you say? The gang-leader might have been able to do something, but he wasn't there. And Shukhov did not say anything to anybody, not wishing to anger The Tartar. He knew that they would keep his breakfast for him.

11

And the two of them went out.

The foggy, bitter cold made you catch your breath. Two large searchlights swept across the parade ground from the far corner watch-towers. The lights on the perimeter, and those inside the camp, were all on. There were so many of them that they completely outshone the stars.

Their felt boots crunching on the snow, prisoners were running quickly by, each about his business – to the latrines, to a store-room, to the post-room, to the kitchen to hand in meals to be individually cooked. All had their heads pressed into their shoulders, their coats buttoned up, and all felt the cold not so much on account of the frost as of the realisation that they would have to spend the entire day in it. But The Tartar in his old greatcoat with the dirty blue tabs walked on steadily, as though quite impervious to the cold.

They walked past the high wooden fence around the stone-built prison block within the camp; past the barbed wire which guarded the camp bakery from the inmates; past the corner of the staff barracks where the frost-covered rail (used to sound reveille) was fixed to a post by thick wire; past another post where – in a sheltered place to prevent it falling too low – hung the thermometer, coated over with frost. Shukhov cast a hopeful sideways glance at the milk-white tube: if it had shown –41, they should not be sent out to work. But today it wasn't even approaching –40.

They went into the staff barracks – straight to the warders' room. There it became clear – as Shukhov had already suspected on the way – that he wasn't going to get punished after all, but that, simply, the floor of the warders' room needed cleaning. The Tartar explained to Shukhov that he was going to let him off, and ordered him to scrub the floor.

Scrubbing the floor in the warders' room was the job of a special prisoner, who was not sent outside the camp to work – the staff barracks' orderly. He had long since sorted things out for himself in the staff barracks; he had access to the offices of the Major, the chief disciplinary officer and the security officer. While serving them, he from time to time heard things which even the warders did not know, and for some time he had reckoned that to scrub floors for ordinary warders was somewhat beneath him. He had been summoned once or twice by the warders for this purpose, but they had grown to understand how the land lay there, and had begun to call upon other prisoners to scrub the floors.

The stove in the warders' room was burning fiercely. Two warders, undressed down to their grimy tunics, were playing draughts, and a third, still with his belted sheepskin coat and felt boots on, was asleep on a narrow bench. A bucket and rag stood in the corner.

Shukhov was delighted and thanked The Tartar for letting him off:

"Thank you, Comrade Warder! Now I'll never lie in late again."

The rule here was simple: finish and go. Now that Shukhov had been given some work, his aches and pains had stopped. He took the bucket and, without his mittens – which in his hurry he had forgotten to take from under his pillow, went to the well.

The gang-leaders who had gone to the PPD had collected together near the post, and one of the younger ones, formerly a Hero of the Soviet Union, climbed up the post and wiped the thermometer.

The others shouted their advice from below:

"Only don't breathe on it, or it'll go up."

"Go up? Fucking likely! I won't affect it."

Tyurin, Shukhov's gang's leader, was not there. Shukhov put down the bucket and pushed his hands into his sleeves. He looked on with curiosity.

The man on the pole said hoarsely:

"–27½. Shit!"

And, taking another look to verify this, he jumped down.

"But it's never right – it always lies," someone said. "Why hang up a correct one here?"

The gang-leaders dispersed. Shukhov ran to the well. The frost bit at his ears under his ear-flaps, which were lowered but not tied.

The top of the well was so thickly covered with ice that the bucket would scarcely go through the hole. And the rope was frozen stiff.

His hands numb, he returned to the warders' room with the steaming bucket and thrust his hands into the well water. It warmed him.

The Tartar wasn't there, but there were four warders standing together. They had stopped playing draughts and sleeping and were arguing about how much millet they'd get in January (food supplies were bad in the nearby settlement, and the warders, although ration cards had long since gone out, could buy certain products at a discount which the locals couldn't get).

"Shut the door, you wretch! There's a draught!" shouted one of the warders.

Nothing to gain by getting your felt boots wet in the morning. There was nothing else to change into even if you could run back to barracks. During eight years' detention, Shukhov had experienced many different systems of footwear: he had lived through the winter without felt boots at all, had not even had leather boots – only bast shoes or "Chetezes" (made from rubber tyres). Nowadays the boot situation was looking rosier: in October Shukhov had received – by dint of accompanying the second-in-command of his gang to the store – a pair of sturdy, hard-wearing boots, with room inside for a couple of warm foot-cloths. For a week he went around as proud as punch, kicking his new heels together. And then in December felt boots arrived – and it was good to be alive. Then some devil in the bookkeeping office whispered in the Commandant's ear that felt boots should be given only to those who gave up their other boots. It was not right that a prisoner should

14

have two pairs of boots at the same time. So Shukhov had to make a choice – whether to get through the whole winter in the boots he'd got in October, or to give up those and wear felt boots even when it began to thaw. Such care he had lavished on those new boots received in October, softening the leather with grease! Nothing had been harder to lose in all those eight years than those boots. They had been tossed together into a single, common heap, and he'd never be able to find them again in the spring.

Now Shukhov had an idea. He nimbly got out of his felt boots, stood them in a corner, shoved his foot-cloths into them (his spoon tinkled on the floor: quickly as he had prepared himself for punishment, he hadn't forgotten his spoon) and, barefoot, began to slosh the water right under the warders' felt boots.

"Hey, take it easy, you swine!" one of the warders shouted, lifting his feet onto a chair.

"Rice? Rice's on a different quota, you can't compare rice . . .!"

"How much water are you using, idiot? That's not the way to wash a floor, is it?"

"Comrade Warder, I can't clean it otherwise. The dirt's ingrained . . ."

"Didn't you ever see your woman scrubbing the floor, pig?"

Shukhov straightened up, holding the dripping rag in his hand. He smiled innocently, revealing the gaps in his teeth, thinned out by scurvy at Ust-Izhma in 1943, when he thought he'd been on his last legs. So much so that his bowels had been running blood, and his worn out stomach could not hold anything down. And now only a lisp remained from those times.

"They took me away from my woman, Comrade Warder, in '41. I can't even remember what she was like."

"That's the way they scrub . . . The swine don't know how to do anything and don't want to. They're not

15

worth the bread we give them. We should feed them on shit."

"Anyway, what the fuck's the point in washing the place every day? It only gets damp. Now, look here, 854. Just wipe it over lightly, in order to moisten it a bit, and then get out fast."

"Rice! You can't compare rice with millet!"

Shukhov was smart about getting along . . .

Work – it was like a stick: it had two ends. If you were working for proper people, then give them quality; for a fool, then just pretend to.

Otherwise, everybody would have given up the ghost long ago, that's for sure.

Shukhov wiped the floor-boards, leaving no dry patches, threw the rag behind the stove without bothering to squeeze it out, put on his felt boots by the door, splashed the rest of the water out of the bucket onto the path used by the authorities – and, following the quickest route, hurried past the bath-house and the dark, cold club to the mess-hall.

He still had to get to the infirmary – he was aching all over again. And he still had to avoid being caught by the warder outside the mess-hall: the camp Commandant had given strict orders that prisoners unaccompanied should be picked up and chucked into the cells.

Today there was no crowd, no queue in front of the mess-hall – a rare occasion. He was able to go straight in.

Inside it was as steamy as in the bath-house – what with the frosty air coming through the doors and the steam from the gruel. Members of the gangs were sitting at tables or crowding in the areas between them, waiting for places. Yelling to each other across the crush, two or three workers from each gang were carrying bowls of gruel and porridge on wooden trays and trying to find places for them on the tables. And even so, they don't hear you, the dolts, and upset your tray – and splash, splash! You have a free hand – then give

16

it to them in the neck! That's the way! Don't stand there in the light, looking for something to lick up.

There at the table, before dipping in his spoon, a young man was crossing himself. That meant a Western Ukrainian – and a new arrival.

The Russians – they had forgotten which hand to cross themselves with.

It was cold sitting in the mess-hall, and most men ate with their caps on, but not hurrying, picking out rotten little bits of fish from under the black cabbage leaves and spitting the bones out on the table. When there was a pile of bones on the table – and before a new gang came to sit down, someone would sweep the bones off, and there, on the floor, they'd be ground underfoot.

To spit the bones directly onto the floor was considered to be bad manners.

In the middle of the mess-hall ran two rows of supporting posts, and near one of these posts sat Fetyukov, a member of Shukhov's gang, who had kept his breakfast for him. Fetyukov was one of the least members of the gang, counting for even less than Shukhov. Externally, all the members of the gang were the same in status – the same black coats and numbers – but beneath there were sharp distinctions. You wouldn't get Buinovsky to look after your bowl for you, and Shukhov would not take on any old job either.

Fetyukov caught sight of Shukhov and sighed as he gave up his place.

"It's all cold. I was going to eat it for you. I thought you were in the cells."

He didn't bother to wait, knowing that there would be nothing left from Shukhov's bowl – that both the bowls he had collected would be scraped clean.

Shukhov pulled his spoon out of his boot. The spoon was dear to him, and had been with him all over the North. He had cast it himself in sand from aluminium

17

wire. There was an inscription on it: "Ust-Izhma, 1944".

Then he took off his cap from his clean-shaven head – however cold it might be, he couldn't bring himself to eat with his cap on – and, stirring the now cold gruel, took a quick look to see what was in the bowl. A medium haul. It had not been poured from the top of the cauldron, nor from the bottom either. Fetyukov wouldn't be above pinching a potato while he was guarding the bowl.

The only decent thing about the gruel was that it was usually hot, but Shukhov's had grown completely cold. However, he began to eat it as slowly and deliberately as always. No need to hurry – even if the roof caught fire. Not counting sleep, a prisoner lived for himself only for ten minutes in the morning at breakfast, five at the lunch break and five at supper.

The gruel did not change from day to day – it depended on the type of vegetable stored for use in the winter. Last year it was salted carrots – which meant nothing but carrots in the gruel from September to June. And this year – black cabbage. The most satisfying time of the year for the prisoner was June, out of season for vegetables, when they substituted groats. The worst time was July: shredded nettles in the cauldron.

Bones were mostly all that remained of the fish, the meat having been boiled off the bones and reduced to nothing except for odd bits on the head and tail. Not leaving a single scale or the tiniest piece of meat on the brittle skeleton, Shukhov still crunched his teeth, sucked the bones dry – and then spat them out onto the table. He ate everything of a fish – the gills, the tail, the eyes, when they had not fallen out of their sockets but when they had been boiled out and floated separately in the bowl – great fish-eyes! – then he did not eat them. He was laughed at for that.

Today Shukhov economised: because he hadn't been back to the barracks, he had not received his bread

18

ration, and now he ate without bread. The bread – he would be able to eat that later; it could even be more satisfying.

After the gruel there was magara porridge. That had frozen into a single, solid lump, and Shukhov had to break it into little pieces. It was not only that the porridge was cold – even when hot, it was tasteless, and quite unfilling: it was just grass, only yellow and looked like millet. They had had the idea of giving them it instead of groats. It was said to come from China. 300 grams of it boiled a day – that was the ration. It certainly wasn't porridge, but it passed for porridge.

Licking his spoon and returning it to the same place in his felt boot, Shukhov put on his cap and set off for the infirmary.

The sky was still quite black, and it was impossible to see the stars for the lights of the camp. The broad beams of two searchlights all the time swept the parade ground. When this camp, a "special" camp, had been established, the warders had had a lot of flares of a type used at the front, and if the electricity failed, they let off flares all over the parade ground, white, yellow, red, just as if it were the front. Later they stopped using them. Perhaps they thought it was too expensive?

It was just as dark as it was at reveille, but to the experienced eye it was easily apparent from various small signs that they would soon be called out on parade.

Khromoi's assistant (Khromoi was the mess-orderly who was able to feed and keep an assistant out of his own pocket) went off to summon Barracks 6 – occupied by those who were sick and did not leave the camp – to breakfast. An old artist with a little beard shuffled towards the Culture and Education Section (CES) to fetch paint and a brush with which to paint the numbers on prison uniforms. Once again The Tartar strode rapidly across the parade-ground in the direction of the staff barracks. Generally speaking, there

19

were not so many people about – which meant that everybody had gone to cover and were warming themselves up during these last sweet minutes.

Shukhov was shrewd enough to hide from The Tartar behind a corner of the barracks – if he got caught again, he really would be for it. It was essential not to get yourself spotted alone by a single one of the warders – stick to the crowd. Maybe he was on the lookout for someone to do a job, or on whom to vent his ill-temper. They had posted up a new order in the barracks that you had to take off your cap to a warder five paces before passing him and put it on again two paces after. Some of the warders wandered around like blind men, not caring a damn, but for others the new order was a real bonus. The number of prisoners who had been slapped in the cells on account of their caps. Oh no, safer to stay round the corner.

The Tartar passed by, and Shukhov finally made up his mind definitely to go to the infirmary – when it occurred to him that surely it was this morning that the tall Latvian from Barracks 7 had told him to come before parade to buy a couple of jars of home-grown tobacco. And it had gone clean out of his head he'd been in such a bustle. The tall Latvian had received a parcel the previous evening, and perhaps there would be no tobacco left by tomorrow, and then he would have to wait a whole month before the Latvian got a new parcel. The Latvian's tobacco was good, strong-flavoured and good to smell and brownish in colour.

Shukhov felt put out and stopped in his tracks – should he not go to Barracks 7? But he was now so close to the infirmary that he jogged up the steps. The snow crunched under his feet.

Inside the hospital, the corridor was, as usual, so clean that he was afraid to step on the floor. The walls were painted with a white enamel paint; and all the furniture was white as well.

But the office doors were all shut. The doctors could

20

not yet have got out of bed. In the orderly room, a medical assistant – a young man called Kolya Vdovushkin – sat behind a clean little table, wearing a shining white coat; he was writing something.

There was nobody else around.

Shukhov took off his cap as, if in front of one of the authorities and, in accepted camp fashion, letting his eyes slide where they had no business, he could not help noticing that Nikolai was writing in beautifully straight lines, each line set in from the edge of the paper and beginning, one below the other, with a capital letter. Shukhov understood immediately, of course, that this was not work, but something private and none of his business.

"Look here, Nikolai Semyonitch, I'm feeling ... sort of ... sick," Shukhov said somewhat shamefully, as if trying to claim something he had no right to.

Vdovushkin looked up from his work, calm and wide-eyed. There were no numbers visible on his white cap and his white coat.

"Why are you so late? Why didn't you come yesterday evening? Don't you know that we can't see people in the morning? The sick-list has already gone to the PPD."

All this Shukhov knew. And he knew that it was not any more simple to get on the sick-list in the evening.

"But, Kolya ... in the evening, when it should have ... it didn't ache."

"But what is it? What is it that aches?"

"Well, when you think about it, nothing does. I just feel bad all over."

Shukhov was not one of those who hung about the infirmary, and Vdovushkin knew that. But he was permitted to put only two men on the sick-list in the morning – and he had already done that, and the names of these two were already written down under the greenish glass of the table with a line drawn beneath them.

21

"You should have thought of that earlier. What do you think you are up to – coming here just before parade? Come on, then."

Vdovushkin took a thermometer from a jar from which a number of thermometers projected through a gauze covering, wiped it and gave it to Shukhov.

Shukhov sat down on a bench near the wall, right at the very edge of it, only not so that it would overturn with him. He did not choose this uncomfortable position on purpose, but as an involuntary expression that the infirmary was unfamiliar to him and that his purpose was unimportant.

Vdovushkin went on writing.

The infirmary was in the most remote corner of the camp, and no sounds could be heard from outside. No clocks ticked here – the prisoners were not permitted to carry watches; the authorities told the time for them. Even the mice did not scratch – they'd all been caught by the hospital cat, designated for that purpose.

It was strange for Shukhov to sit in such a clean room, in such quietness, under a bright light with nothing to do for a full five minutes. He gazed at all the walls – but found nothing there. He looked at his jacket – the number on his chest had become indistinct and would have to be renewed if he were to keep out of trouble. With his free hand he felt the beard on his face – quite a stubble had grown since his last bath more than ten days previously. But he didn't mind that. He would be having another bath in about three days' time, and he could shave then. No point in waiting in the barber's queue. He didn't have to beautify himself for anybody.

Then, looking at Vdovushkin's gleaming white cap, Shukhov remembered the hospital on the banks of the river Lovat, how he had arrived there with an injured jaw and – fool that he was! – of his own free will returned to the front. And he could have had five days in bed.

And now he dreamed of going sick for two or three

weeks, not fatally or anything requiring an operation, but just that he could be sent to the hospital – and be able to lie there for three weeks without moving, and even if the hospital food was pretty meagre – it didn't matter.

But Shukhov remembered that now you couldn't even lie back in the camp hospital. A new doctor had shown up from some or other transport centre for prisoners – Stepan Grigoritch, a busy, loud-voiced man who gave neither himself nor his patients any peace: he had had the idea of sending all those patients who could actually walk out to work around the hospital – making fences, laying paths, carrying soil to the flower-beds; and in winter, there was snow to clear. He was always saying that work was the most effective cure for illness.

But many a horse has died of overwork. He should have understood that. If he'd spent a bit of time laying blocks, he would keep his mouth shut, for sure.

Vdovushkin continued to write. He was, indeed, doing something "on the side", but it didn't matter to Shukov. He was writing out a new, long poem he'd completed the previous day, and today he had promised to show it to Stepan Grigoritch, the very same doctor who championed work as a therapy for illness.

As can only happen in prison camps, Stepan Grigoritch had advised Vdovushkin to describe himself as a medical assistant, and Vdovushkin had begun to learn to give intravenous injections to ignorant prisoners, on whose simple minds it would never dawn that a medical assistant might not be a medical assistant at all. In fact, Kolya was a student of literature who had been arrested in his second year. Stepan Grigoritch was keen that he should write in prison what he had not been in a position to write as a free man.

The signal for parade was scarcely audible through the double windows, made opaque by the thick, white frost. Shukhov sighed and stood up. He felt as feverish

23

as before, but it was clear that he would not be able to get off work. Vdovushkin reached for the thermometer and looked at it.

"Look, it's neither one thing nor the other – it's under ninety-nine. If it were a hundred, there would be no problem. But I can't hold you as sick. You can stay at your own risk if you want. If the doctor considers you're ill, he'll let you off; but if not, it'll be the cells for you. You'd do better to go to work."

Shukhov made no reply, didn't even nod, but pulled his cap over his eyes and went out.

There's no point in expecting someone who's warm to understand someone who's cold.

The cold was oppressive. A biting, foggy chill enveloped Shukhov and made him cough raspingly. The temperature was –27, and Shukhov's was ninety-nine. It was one against the other.

Shukhov made no reply, didn't even nod, but pulled ground was quite deserted, and the camp looked empty. It was that short moment before parade when it was possible to imagine, against all the odds, that there would not even be a parade. The escort guards were sitting in their warm quarters, their sleepy heads propped against their rifles – it was not all clover for them either, shilly-shallying on the watch-towers in such cold. The guards at the main gate threw coal into the stove. The warders in the warders' room were finishing their last cigarettes before going out to search the barracks. And the prisoners, now got up in all their rags, held together with pieces of string, their faces wrapped in rags from chin to eyes as protection against the cold, were lying on top of the blankets on their bunks with their felt boots on, their eyes closed, just waiting in trepidation for the gang-leader to cry out: "All out!"

Gang 104, along with the rest of Barracks 9, were dozing – except for the second-in-command Pavlo, whose lips moved as he counted something up with a small pencil; and on the top bunk, the Baptist Alyoshka,

24

Shukhov's neighbour, was reading his notebook, in which he had copied half the Gospels.

Shukhov ran into the barracks without a sound, and went up to the second-in-command's bunk.

Pavlo looked up.

"So you're not in the cells, Ivan Denisovitch? Still alive?" (The Western Ukrainians would never change, even in the camp they addressed people by their patronymic.)

Taking Shukhov's bread ration from the table, he handed it to him. On top of the bread lay a little heap of sugar.

Shukhov was in a great hurry, but nevertheless he responded respectfully (a second-in-command was really a kind of official, and one depended upon him even more than upon the Commandant of the camp). Despite his haste, he sucked up the sugar from the bread with his lips, licking with his tongue as he levered himself up with one leg to make his bed, all the while inspecting his ration of bread, weighing it in his hand to see if it constituted the full 550 grams that was his due. Shukhov had received thousands of similar rations in prisons and camps, and although he had never been in a position to weigh one of them on a pair of scales, and although he had always hesitated to defend his rights, did not know, timid as he was, how to, it had long been evident to him and every other prisoner that there was no such thing as honesty in the apportioning of the bread ration. There was no ration that was not short – the point was, how short? So you inspected it every day, to ease your mind – perhaps you hadn't been too badly treated today? Perhaps you had received almost your full quota?

"About twenty grams under," Shukhov determined, and broke the bread in two. One half he shoved under his jacket, into a little white pocket he had specially sewn (prisoners' jackets were made at the factory without pockets). The other half, which he had saved by not

25

getting his ration until after breakfast, he considered eating there and then, but food eaten in a hurry is no food at all, is no good and does not give satisfaction. He began to put half the bread into his locker, but thought about it again; he remembered that two orderlies had been beaten up for pinching. The barracks was big, like a public courtyard.

So, his hands still grasping the bread, Ivan Denisovitch withdrew his feet from his felt boots, deftly leaving his foot-cloths and spoon within, climbed barefoot up to his bunk, widened a little hole in his mattress and there, amidst the sawdust, he hid his piece of bread. He took off his cap, pulled out a needle and thread from it (hidden deeply, because they did not neglect to examine your cap when they searched you; once a warder had pricked himself on a needle and had almost knocked Shukhov's head off in his rage). Stitch, stitch, stitch, and the little hole was sewn up with the bread concealed. Meanwhile, the sugar in his mouth had melted. Every nerve in Shukhov's body was strained to breaking-point – at any moment the warder at the door would begin yelling. Shukhov's fingers moved rapidly, but his mind, racing ahead, was reckoning the next move. Alyoshka the Baptist was reading the Gospels not just to himself but almost out loud (perhaps for Shukhov's benefit, those Baptists loved to evangelise):

"But let no one of you suffer as a murderer, or as a thief, or as an evildoer, or interfering in the affairs of other men. But if you suffer as a Christian, then do not be ashamed – but glorify God on that behalf."

Alyoshka was crafty: he had been so skilful at concealing his little book in a hole in the wall that it had survived every search.

With the same rapid movements, Shukhov hung up his coat on the cross-beam, and pulled out from under the mattress his mittens, a pair of thin foot-cloths, a piece of string and a rag with tapes at each end. He evened out the sawdust in the mattress (it was heavy

26

and thickly packed), tucked in the blanket all round, arranged the pillow – and then clambered down bare-foot and began to wrap his feet, first with the good foot-cloths, which were new, then the bad, torn ones.

Then the gang-leader hoicked, got up and bawled:

"No more sleep, 104. Outside!"

And immediately everyone in the gang, whether they had been dozing or not, got up, yawned and made for the door. The gang-leader had nineteen years' experience, and he wouldn't call you out for parade a moment before it was necessary. When he said "Outside!", he meant it, and there was no time to lose.

And while the men, with heavy tread, without a word, went out one after another first into the corridor, then through the doorway onto the steps, and the leader of Gang 20, just like Tyurin, shouted: "Outside!" Shuk-hov hurriedly put on his felt boots over the two layers of foot-cloths, put his coat over his jacket and tied it tightly with rope (leather belts had been disallowed in "special" camps).

Shukhov succeeded in finishing everything he had to do and caught up with the last of his gang-members at the doorway – as their numbered backs moved through the doorway onto the steps. Bulky, dressed in everything they had by way of clothing, the men progressed diagonally, in single file towards the parade-ground, no-body in a hurry to get there first. They moved heavily, their boots crunching in the snow – that was the only noise.

It was still dark, although the sky in the east was beginning to brighten and to take on a greenish tint. A light, sharp little wind was blowing also from the east.

There was nothing more bitter than this moment – going out on parade in the morning. In the dark, in the cold, with an empty belly, to face the day. You lose your tongue, you don't want to speak to anyone.

A junior warder was rushing about the parade-ground.

"Well, Tyurin, how long must we wait for you? Shirking again?"

Shukhov might have been frightened of this young warder, but not Tyurin. He wasn't going to waste his breath on him in this cold, just trudged on in silence. And the gang followed him through the snow: tramp, tramp, crunch, crunch.

Tyurin must have slipped the officials that pound of lard, because it was evident from the position of other gangs that Gang 104 was going again to its usual place in the column. They'd be sending one of the poorer, less crafty gangs to the Socialist Community Centre. Oh, it'd be hell there today: −27 and a wind, and no shelter and no fire!

The gang-leader needed a lot of lard – to be able to slip it to the PPD officials as well as satisfy his own belly. Tyurin himself never received any parcels – yet he was never short of lard. Any member of the gang receiving some handed it over to Tyurin immediately.

That was the way to survive.

The senior warder recorded something on a little board.

"Tyurin, you've got one man sick today, and twenty-three fit for work, is that it?"

"Twenty-three," the gang-leader said with a nod.

Who was missing? Pantaleyev was not present. Was he sick then?

And immediately there was whispering among the gang: Pantaleyev, the son of a bitch, was staying behind again. He wasn't sick at all – the security people were keeping him back. He'd be splitting on somebody again.

They could summon him during the day without any trouble, keep him for three hours, and no one would know or hear.

They fixed it through the infirmary . . .

The parade-ground was black with prisoners' coats as the gangs shuffled forward across it to be searched. Shukhov remembered that he had wanted to renew the

28

numbers on his jacket, and elbowed his way to the side of the parade-ground. There, two or three prisoners were waiting in turn in front of the artist. Shukhov joined them. Those numbers meant nothing but trouble – if you did something wrong, a warder could spot you by your number at a distance, and he would write your number down. And if you didn't have your number renewed, then into the cells you went for not looking after it properly.

There were three artists in the camp. They painted pictures free for the authorities, and took it in turns to be present at parade. Today it was an old man with a grey beard. When he painted the number on your cap, it was like being anointed by a priest on your brow.

He painted and painted, occasionally blowing into his glove. It was a thin, knitted glove, and his hand grew stiff with cold so that he could scarcely manage to form the numbers.

The artist renewed the "S–854" on Shukhov's jacket, and Shukhov, the rope for tightening around his coat in his hand and his coat loose – the searchers were nearby – caught up with his gang. And at once he noticed that another member of his gang, Tsesar, was smoking, not a pipe but a cigarette – which meant that he might have been able to cadge a smoke. But Shukhov did not ask him direct, stood quite close to him and, half turning, looked past him.

He looked past him with an air of indifference, but he saw how after each drag (Tsesar was thinking and only rarely dragged on the cigarette) the circle of red ash moved down the cigarette, shortening it as it crept towards the holder.

Just then that jackal, Fetyukov, came up and stood directly opposite Tsesar, watching his mouth with burning eyes.

Shukhov did not have a scrap of tobacco left, and today saw no prospect of getting any before the evening. He was tense all over in expectation, and now all his desire was concentrated on that dog-end, for which he felt he would be ready to give his freedom – but he wouldn't lower himself like Fetyukov, he wouldn't look at someone's mouth.

Tsesar was a mixture of many nationalities: you couldn't tell whether he was a Greek, a Jew or a Gypsy. He was still a young man. He used to make films. But he had not completed his first when he was arrested. He had a thick, black, bushy moustache. It hadn't been shaved off in the camp because that is how he appeared in the official photograph they had of him.

"Tsesar Markovitch," Fetyukov slobbered, unable to restrain himself. "Give us a drag, then!"

His face twitched with greed and desire.

Tsesar raised his eyelids a little – they were half-lowered over his black eyes – and looked at Fetyukov. He had begun to smoke a pipe more often than before because that way people wouldn't keep cadging from him whenever he smoked. It wasn't the tobacco he grudged, but his thoughts being interrupted. He smoked in order to set his mind thinking and to stimulate ideas in himself. But scarcely would he have lit a cigarette than he would instantly see in a number of eyes: "Leave me the dog-end."

Tsesar turned to Shukhov and said:

"Take it, Ivan Denisovitch."

And with his thumb he pushed the burning end out of the short amber holder.

Shukhov gave a start (although he had been expecting Tsesar to do as he had done), with one hand hurriedly – and gratefully – took the end, and put his other hand underneath in case it fell. He was not offended that Tsesar felt squeamish about giving him the cigarette to finish in the holder (some people had clean mouths, some foul), and his hardened fingers did not suffer as he held it right up to the burning end. The main thing was that he had beaten that jackal Fetyukov to it, and here he was now puffing away until his lips began to burn.

Mmmm ... The smoke pervaded his hungry body, and seemed to penetrate into his feet and head.

Just as that blissful feeling spread over his body, Ivan Denisovitch heard the shout:

"They're taking off our undershirts!"

Such was the life of a prisoner. Shukhov had grown accustomed to it: only watch out that they didn't go for your throat.

Why undershirts? Undershirts had been issued by the Commandant himself. No, something wasn't right ...

There were two gangs ahead of them waiting to be searched, and everyone in Gang 104 looked about: the chief disciplinary officer, Lieutenant Volkovoi, had come from the staff barracks and shouted something to the warders. And the warders, who had done their searching in quite a slapdash way until Volkovoi came on the scene, now set to with a vengeance and hurled themselves into the job like wild animals.

"Open your undershirts!" a senior warder yelled.

It was said that the Commandant himself – quite apart from the prisoners and the warders – was frightened of Volkovoi. God had named the rogue well.* Wolf he was, and he looked it. Dark and tall and scowling – and rapid in his movements. He'd emerge from behind a barracks with: "What's going on here?" One couldn't keep out of his way. At first he had carried a whip of braided leather, as thick as his arm. They said he beat people with it in the cells. Or he'd creep up behind someone, when the prisoners were collected together by the barracks for the evening count, and lash his neck with the whip. "Why aren't you standing in line, you swine?" The group would retreat from him like a receding wave. The man struck by the whip would clasp his neck, wipe away the blood and keep his mouth shut – in case he got shoved in the cells as well.

Now, for some reason, he had stopped carrying the whip.

* Volk means wolf in Russian.

31

In the freezing weather, the search routine was not so rigorous in the morning – although it remained so in the evening. The prisoners untied their coats and held the skirts open. They went up by fives, and five warders awaited them. They felt with their hands inside the jackets of the prisoners, slapped the only pocket they were allowed to have – on the right knee, and because they didn't want to take off their gloves, if they came across anything unusual, they wouldn't get hold of it immediately, but ask, not hurrying: "What do we have here?"

What did they expect to find on a prisoner in the morning? Knives? But knives were not taken out of the camp, but brought in. In the morning it was necessary to make sure that a prisoner was not carrying a large amount of food out with him, with the purpose of escaping with it. There was a time when they were so frightened of the 200-gram chunks of bread the prisoners would take to eat with their dinner that an order was issued for each gang to make for themselves a wooden box in which all the bread of the gang, collected from each of its members, would be carried. It was impossible to guess how they sought to benefit by such an arrangement – most likely it was to torment, to make excessive work. You had to take a bite out of your bit of bread, and make your mark on it as it were, and then put it in the box; but pieces of bread are exactly alike, and they were all from the same loaf – and all along the way to work you thought about your bit and worried about it, whether your bit would get taken by somebody else, and sometimes there were quarrels among friends to the point of fighting. Then one day three men escaped from the construction site in a truck, taking such a box of bread with them. Then the authorities collected their senses, and all the boxes were chopped up in the guard-room. From now on, each to carry his own bit of bread.

In the morning they also had to ascertain that no one

was wearing civilian clothes under the camp uniform. But then everybody had had all his civilian things long ago removed from him, and had been told that he would not get them back until the end of his sentence. In this camp nobody had yet completed his sentence.

And they also kept an eye out for letters which might have been mailed through someone outside the camp. But if they were going to search for every letter, they'd be there until dinner-time.

But Volkovoi shouted that they were to search for something – and so the warders quickly took off their gloves, ordered the men to open up their jackets (where each man had preserved some of the warmth from his barracks) and unbutton their undershirts, and ran up and down, feeling to see whether they were wearing anything against the regulations. Each prisoner was allowed two shirts – a shirt and an undershirt – and anything else was to be removed. That was Volkovoi's order, which was passed among the prisoners from rank to rank. The gangs which had already been searched – they were lucky, and some had already gone through the gates; but the rest had to strip themselves. And anyone with more than the regulation amount of clothes on had there and then, in the cold, to give it up!

That's how it began, but trouble soon came of it: the flow of men through the gates eased up, and the escort guards began to shout: "Come on, come on!" So Gang 104 didn't suffer as much as they might have done from Volkovoi; and the warders were told to write down the names of anyone with extra clothing on – and such people were to report to the store-room that evening with a written explanation as to how and why they had concealed extra clothes.

Shukhov was dressed according to regulations – feel me all over then, there's only my soul in my chest. But they wrote down that Tsesar had got on a flannel shirt, and Buinovsky had some kind of waistcoat or jerkin. Buinovsky, who had not been in the camp three

33

months and who was accustomed to life on board, objected:

"You've no right to make people undress in the cold! You don't know Article Nine of the Criminal Code!"

But they did have the right and they knew the article. It's you, brother, who doesn't know yet.

"You're not true Soviets!" the captain went on. "You're not Communists."

Volkovoi had tolerated talk of the Criminal Code, but now, like black lightning, he flashed back:

"Ten days inside!"

And more quietly to the senior warder:

"You can arrange it this evening."

They didn't like putting people in the cells in the morning, because it meant the loss of a day's work. Let him break his back all day, and be put inside in the evening.

The prison block was to the left of the parade ground – a stone building with two wings. They had finished building the second wing in the autumn – the authorities had run out of room in the first. The prison had eighteen cells, as well as others, set apart, for solitary confinement. The rest of the camp was made of wood, only the prison block of stone.

The cold had got under the prisoners' undershirts, and now it wouldn't go away. It had been pointless for the prisoners to wrap themselves up. Shukhov's back was aching already. Oh, to be lying down in a hospital bed just now – and to sleep. There was nothing he wanted more. Under a really heavy blanket.

The prisoners were standing in front of the gates buttoning and tying themselves up, and the escort guards were shouting from outside the gates:

"Come on, come on!"

And a warder was jostling them in the back:

"Come on, come on!"

The first gates. The perimeter. The second gates. Railings along both sides by the guard-room.

"Halt!" one of the guards yelled. "Just like a flock of sheep! Line up in fives!"

It was beginning to grow light. Beyond the guard-room, the escort guards' fire was burning itself out. They always lit a fire before parade – to warm them-selves and in order to be able to see to count.

One of the guards counted in a loud, shrill voice:
"One, two, three!"

The men had separated into groups of five, and each group marched forward on its own so that whichever way you looked at it, you saw five heads, five backs, ten legs.

A second guard stood silently by the railings, only making sure that the count was right.

And a lieutenant from the camp stood and watched.

Each man was dearer than gold to a guard. If you found yourself with one head too few, then your own head was likely to make up the difference.

And again the gang formed up all together.

And now an escort guard began to count them off:
"One, two, three!"

Again the men separated by fives and marched for-ward.

And the assistant to the Chief Escort Guard counted them in on the other side.

As did another lieutenant – from outside the camp.

No mistakes could be made. If you signed for one head too many, then you also made it up with your own head.

There were escort guards everywhere. They formed a semi-circle round the column going to the power-station, shouldered their tommy guns and pointed them right in your face. And there were dog-handlers with grey dogs. One dog bared its teeth as though it were laughing at the prisoners. The escort guards all wore short sheepskin coats, except for six wearing long coats. The long coats could be changed among the guards;

35

they were worn by those deputed to man the watch-towers.

Once more, bringing the gangs together, the escort guards counted by fives the column heading for the power-station.

"It's always coldest at dawn," Buinovsky explained. "Because that is the last stage of the cooling process which takes place at night."

The captain liked to explain things. He could work out for you the particular phase of the moon – whether it was old or new – for any day of any year.

The captain was deteriorating before your very eyes. His cheeks were sunken – but he kept cheerful.

The cold here outside the camp, with a strong wind blowing, bit even Shukhov's face, used as it was to almost anything. Realising that he would have the wind in his face all the way to the power-station, he decided to don his piece of rag. Like many others, he had a piece of rag with two long tapes to use when the wind was against him. The prisoners admitted that such a rag could help. Shikhov covered his face up to his eyes, passed the tapes around below his ears and tied them behind his neck. Then he covered the back of his neck with the flap of his cap and raised his coat collar. Then he pulled the front flap of his cap down over his fore-head. And so in front only his eyes were naked to the wind. He tightened his coat firmly at the waist with the rope. Now everything was fine except for his mittens, which were thin, and his hands had already begun to freeze. He rubbed them and clapped them together, knowing that soon he would have to put them behind his back and leave them there for the rest of the way.

The Chief Escort Guard read the daily "sermon" of which every prisoner was heartily sick:

"Attention, prisoners! Column order on the march will be strictly observed. No straggling or racing, no changing from one group of five to another, no talking, you will look to the front at all times and keep your hands behind your back. A step to the right or left is considered an attempt at escape, and the escort guard will open fire without warning. Leading ranks, quick march!"

The two escort guards at the head of the column must have started out along the road. The column in front began to sway, shoulders began to swing, and guards, twenty paces to the right and left of the column and ten paces separating one from the next, moved forward, tommy guns at the ready.

There hadn't been any snow for a week, and the road was well-trodden and smooth. They circuited the camp, and the wind caught them sideways on. Hands clenched behind their backs, heads lowered, the column moved forward as if to a funeral. All you could see was the feet of two or three people ahead of you and the piece of trodden ground where your own feet went. From time to time one of the escort guards would shout: "U–48! Hands behind your back!" "B–502! Keep up!" Then the shouts became more rare: the wind whipped at them, and it was difficult to see. The escort guards were not allowed to tie cloths round their faces. It wasn't much fun for them either.

When it was warmer, everyone in the column talked no matter how much they were shouted at. But today everyone was hunched forward, each man hiding behind the back of the one in front of him, thinking his own thoughts.

Even the thoughts of a prisoner are not free, always returning to the same thing, turning it over in his mind again and again: would they find that piece of bread in his mattress? Will the infirmary put me on the sick-list this evening? Will they put the captain in the cells or not? And how did Tsesar get hold of that warm flannel shirt? He must have bribed someone in the store-room for people's private possessions, how else?

Because he had breakfasted without bread and his food had been cold, Shukhov felt quite empty today.

37

And in order to stop his belly from grumbling and begging for food, he stopped thinking about the camp, but thought instead about the letter he would soon be writing home.

The column passed by the wood-factory which had been built by the prisoners, went past a block of living-quarters also built by the prisoners but housing free workers, past the new club (again, built from the foundations to the wall decorations by the prisoners – but it was the free workers who watched the films there), and the column moved out on to the steppe, straight into the wind and into the reddening dawn. Bare white snow lay in every direction, and there wasn't a single tree to be seen.

A new year had begun, '51, and Shukhov had the right to send two letters during that year. He had sent his last letter in July and had received an answer in October. At Ust-Izhma, the system had been different – there you could write every month. But what can you write in a letter? Shukhov had written no more frequently there than he did now.

Shukhov had left home on June 23rd, 1941. The previous Sunday, people had come back from Mass at Polomnya and reported that the war had started. They had learned about it in the post-office at Polomnya; in Temgenovo there had been no wireless sets before the war. Now, they wrote, "piped" radio blared out of every hut.

Writing now was like throwing stones into a bottomless pool. They sank without trace – and that was the last you heard. There was no point in writing to say which gang you were working in, and what sort of gang-leader Andrei Prokofyevitch Tyurin was. Right now he had more to say to Kilgas the Latvian than to his family.

And from the two letters a year they wrote him, you couldn't tell much about their lives. A new chairman of the kolkhoz – as if that didn't happen every year!

The kolkhoz had been merged – but such mergers had taken place before, and then un-mergers. Or else somebody had failed to carry out his work quota, and had had his private plot reduced to 1,500 square metres, and someone else had lost it altogether.

What Shukhov could never take in was that, according to his wife, there hadn't been a single addition to the kolkhoz since the war: all the young men and women did all they could to work in the factories in the town or in the peat-works. Half the men had not returned from the war at all, and those who had did not want to have anything to do with the kolkhoz: they lived at home but worked outside the kolkhoz. The only men in the kolkhoz were the gang-leader Zakhar Vasilyitch and the carpenter, Tikhon, who was eighty-four and had recently married – and already had children. It was the women who had been there since '30 who held the place together.

This was something Shukhov couldn't understand at all: to live on the kolkhoz but work elsewhere. Shukhov had seen life on individual and collective farms, but men not working in their own village – that he couldn't take. Did they do seasonal work? And what about the haymaking?

They had stopped seasonal work a long time before, his wife answered. They didn't go out carpentering, for which that part was famous; they didn't make baskets any more, because nobody wanted them nowadays. But there was a new craft, a cheerful one it seemed – painting carpets. Someone had brought back some stencils from the war, and from that time it became more and more popular, and there were a great many skilled workers at it. They did not have any regular employment, they worked nowhere in particular, and helped the kolkhoz for only one month in the year, at the time of haymaking and harvesting; and to cover the other eleven, they got a chit from the kolkhoz saying that so-and-so was released from kolkhoz work to carry on his own affairs and was not subject to taxes. And they travelled all over the country and even flew in aeroplanes to save time, piling up thousands of roubles and painting carpets everywhere: fifty roubles a carpet they got, made out of some old sheet – and it didn't take more than an hour to do just one. And his wife very much hoped that when Ivan returned, he also would become one of these painters. They'd be able to raise themselves out of the poverty she was suffering, send the children to technical school and build themselves a new hut in place of the rotten old one they had now. All the painters were building themselves new houses, and near the railway-station the cost of a house had risen from 5,000 to 25,000 roubles.

Then he asked his wife how he was going to become a painter – he who had never been able to draw in his life? And what was so marvellous about these carpets, anyway? His wife replied that any old fool could paint the carpets: all you had to do was put the stencil in position and paint through the little holes with a brush. And there were three types of carpet: "Troika" – an officer of the Hussars driving a beautiful carriage drawn by three horses; two, "The Red Deer"; and the third had a Persian design. There were no other designs, but people all over the country were only too glad to get their hands on these. Because a real carpet doesn't cost fifty roubles, but thousands.

Shukhov would have loved to see those carpets ...

In all his time in camps and prisons, Ivan Denisovitch had lost the habit of concerning himself about the next day, or the next year, or about feeding his family. The authorities did all his thinking for him, and, somehow, it was easier like that. He still had another two summers and winters to serve. But those carpets irritated him ...

It was clearly an easy way to make money, you see. And it wouldn't be right if he did not keep pace with the other villagers ... But in his heart Ivan Denisovitch did not really want to become a carpet-painter. You had to have a lot of confidence and cheek for that, know how to grease the right palm. Shukhov had been walking this earth for forty years, had only half his teeth and was getting bald, but he had never either given or taken a bribe, and hadn't learnt to do so in the camp either.

Easy money – it weighs nothing and doesn't give you the feeling that you have worked for it. The old adage was right: what you don't pay for, you don't get value for. Shukhov's hands could still be put to good use, and surely he would find work when he was free as a stove-maker or a joiner, or a metal-worker?

Only if they didn't give him back his civil rights, and didn't allow him to go home – then he might have to busy himself with those carpets.

Meanwhile the column had come to a halt before the guard-room of the enormous power-station site. A little before, at the corner of the site, two escort guards in sheepskin coats had detached themselves from the column and made off across the country to distant watch-towers. Until guards were occupying all the watch-towers, nobody was allowed inside the site. The Chief Escort Guard, with a tommy gun over his shoulder, went to the guard-room. Smoke billowed out of the guard-room chimney: a civilian guard sat there all night to stop planks and cement being stolen.

Far over on the other side of the site, the sun, big and red and as if in a haze, was rising, its beams cutting sideways across the gates, the whole site area and the distant fence. Alyoshka, standing beside Shukhov, looked at the sun and rejoiced, a smile on his lips. His cheeks were sunken, he lived on his ration alone, never earned anything over and above that – why was he so pleased? Sundays he spent whispering with the other Baptists. The camp did not get them down – it was like water off a duck's back.

On the way, Shukhov's face-cloth had got all wet

from his breath, and in places it had frozen and formed an icy crust. He pulled it down from his face to his neck and stood with his back to the wind. He didn't feel cold everywhere, but his hands were numb in his thin mittens, and the toes of his left foot were frozen: his left boot was in bad shape and would have to be sewn up again.

From the small of his back right to his shoulders, his back ached and throbbed – how could he work?

He looked round, and his eyes fell on the face of the gang-leader, who had been among the last group of five. The gang-leader had powerful shoulders and a broad face. His face was grim. He didn't put up with any fucking games from his gang – but he cared about getting them good rations. He was serving his second term, had spent much of his life in camps, and knew the ropes backwards.

In a camp, the gang-leader means everything: a good one will give you a second life, a bad one will put you in your coffin. Shukhov had known Andrei Prokofyevitch in the days of Ust-Izhma, only hadn't been in his gang there. And when prisoners in under Article 58 had been moved from general camps, such as the one at Ust-Izhma, to penal camps, Tyurin had picked him out. Shukhov had no dealings with the Commandant, the PPD, the work superintendents or the engineers – the gang-leader did all that with his steel chest. In return, he had only to raise an eyebrow or beckon with his finger – and you ran and did what he wanted. You could cheat anyone in the camp, but you didn't cheat Tyurin. You depended on him for your life.

Shukhov wanted to ask the gang-leader whether they were going to work in the same place as yesterday, or whether they were going elsewhere – but he was afraid to interrupt his lofty thoughts. He had only just got them out of going to the Socialist Community Centre, and now he must be pondering the "percentage" the gang should receive, on which their food would depend for the following five days.

42

The gang-leader's face was heavily pock-marked. He stood facing the wind but without moving a muscle; the skin on his face was like the bark of an oak-tree.

In the column the prisoners were rubbing their hands and stamping their feet. What a wicked wind! It appeared as if all six watch-towers were now manned – but they were still not letting them into the site. They badgered the life out of you with their vigilance.

Now! The Chief Escort Guard came out of the guard-room with a checker. They stood on either side of the gates and then opened them.

"Line up in fives! One, two ..."

The prisoners marched as though on parade, nearly in step. Once they were inside the site, they knew what to do.

Just beyond the guard-room was the office, and near the office stood a work-superintendant, indicating to the gang-leaders that they should go to him. Der was there, a foreman but a prisoner himself, a regular bastard who treated his fellow-prisoners worse than dogs.

Eight o'clock, five minutes past (the hooter had just given a blast). The authorities were afraid that the prisoners would waste time, would find warm corners to linger in – but the prisoners had a long day ahead of them and there was plenty of time. As soon as a prisoner enters the site, he bends down to pick up scraps of firewood here and there for the stove – and to hide them away.

Tyurin ordered Pavlo, his second-in-command, to go with him to the office. Tsesar went there as well. Tsesar was rich, got two parcels a month and bribed everybody it was necessary to – he had a soft job in the office, working as the assistant to the norm-checker.

The rest of Gang 104 immediately pushed off.

The sun rose red and hazy over the empty site. There were some panels for prefabs covered with snow; else-where, the beginnings of a brick wall on which work had been abandoned at the foundations; there, the smashed arm of an excavator; a scoop; some scrap-metal. Everywhere there were ditches and trenches and holes. The automobile repair-shops were completed except for the roofs; and, on a rise, the power-station, where work had begun on the second storey.

There was nobody to be seen – except for the six guards in the watch-towers, and people bustling around the office. And this moment was for the prisoners! The Chief Work-Superintendant, it was said, had many times threatened to issue work orders to the gangs the evening before – but it wasn't to be, because by the time the morning came round, they'd changed their minds anyway.

So this was a time for the prisoners! While the authorities were arranging things, you sought out the warmest place you could find and sat back and took it easy – you'd soon be breaking your back, for sure. It was good if you could get near a stove – you could take off your foot-cloths and warm them up a bit. Then your feet would be warm all day. But even without a stove it was still good.

Gang 104 went to the big room in the automobile repair-shops, where they'd paned the windows last autumn and where Gang 38 were making concrete blocks. Some of the blocks lay around in moulds, others, reinforced by mesh, were standing on end. The ceiling was high and the floor was of earth, and it was only warm here because it had been heated with coal – not to warm the men, but so that the blocks would set better. There was even a thermometer, and on Sundays, if for some reason the camp was not working, a free worker would still keep the stove going.

Gang 38, of course, wouldn't let any strangers near the stove, they sat round it themselves, drying their foot-cloths. Well, we'll have to sit in the corner, it's not too bad.

Shukhov found a place for his padded trousers –

where had they not sat? — on the edge of a wooden mould, and leaned back against the wall. And when he leaned back, his coat and jacket tightened, and on the left side of his chest, near his heart, he felt something hard pressing against him. It was the corner of the hunk of bread in his inside pocket, half of his ration that morning which he had taken with him for his dinner. He always took the same amount with him to work and never touched it until dinnertime. But he usually ate the other half at breakfast, and today he hadn't. And Shukhov realised that he had not really economised. He had a great yearning to eat the bread now, in this warm spot. It was five hours until dinner, and that was a long time.

The pain he had felt in his back had now moved to his legs, and they began to feel quite weak. If only he could get them near the stove!

Shukhov placed his mittens on his knees, undid his coat, untied his frozen face-cloth from his neck, folded it several times and put it in his pocket. Then he reached for the hunk of bread in a little white cloth and, holding the cloth against his chest inside his coat so as not to allow a crumb to fall, he began ever so slowly to nibble and chew at the bread. He had carried the bread under two layers of clothes and had warmed it with his own body — so it was not in the least frozen.

In camps Shukhov had often remembered how they used to eat in the village: potatoes by the saucepanful, masses of porridge, and big chunks of meat in the old days. And milk enough to make you burst. Shukhov had learned in camps that that was not the way to eat. You should eat with all your thoughts concentrated on your food, just as now he was nibbling the little pieces of bread, rolling them with his tongue and sucking them into his cheeks — and then it tasted good, this moist black bread. What had he had for eight or nine years? Nothing. And the work he had done on it, well . . .

So was Shukhov occupied with his 200 grams of

bread, and near him, on the same side of the room, sat the remainder of Gang 104.

Two Estonians, who were like blood brothers, sat on a low concrete block, taking it in turns to smoke half a cigarette from a single holder. The Estonians were both fair, tall and thin, and both had long noses and big eyes. They kept so close to each other that it was as if they were obliged to breathe the same air. The gang-leader never separated them. They shared all their food and slept next to each other in top bunks. And when they stood in the column, or waited on parade, or prepared to go to bed at night, all the time they talked to each other in low, unhurried voices. And they were not brothers at all, but had become friends here, in Gang 104. One of them, they explained, had been a fisherman from the coast, the other, when the Soviets established themselves in Estonia, had been taken by his parents as a small child to Sweden. But he had grown up with an independent spirit and had returned to Estonia to finish college.

They say it doesn't matter to which nation you belong, every nation has its share of bad people. But of all the Estonians Shukhov had seen, he had never come across a bad one.

They all sat around – some on the blocks, some on the moulds, some on the ground itself. You didn't feel like talking in the morning, and each one of them was sunk in his own thoughts, silent. That jackal Fetyukov had been collecting dog-ends all over the place (he would take them out of the spitoon, he wasn't fussy), and now he was breaking them up on his knees and pouring the unsmoked tobacco into a piece of paper. Fetyukov had three children at home, but when he had been taken, they had all disassociated themselves from him, and his wife had remarried: so he got no help from anywhere.

Buinovsky kept glancing over at Fetyukov, and then he bawled:

46

"Hey, what are you doing, collecting all kinds of infection? You'll get syphilitic lips! Chuck the stuff away!"

The captain was used to giving orders, and he spoke to everybody in a commanding tone.

But Fetyukov had no reason to depend upon Buinovsky – the captain got no parcels either. And smirking, to show his mouth half empty of teeth, he said:

"You wait until you've been here eight years, Captain, and you'll be picking up dog-ends yourself. Prouder men than you have descended to it in camp ..."

Fetyukov was making the judgement by his own standards. Perhaps the captain would hold out ...

"What's that?" asked Senka Klevshin, who was half-deaf. He thought that the conversation referred to Buinovsky's being caught on parade that morning. "You shouldn't have snapped like that." He shook his head sorrowfully. "It would all have blown over."

Senka Klevshin was a quiet, unfortunate fellow. One of his eardrums had burst in '41. Then he'd been taken prisoner, escaped, had been recaptured and chucked into Buchenwald. In Buchenwald he had managed to stay alive by a miracle, and now he served his sentence quietly. If you kicked up a stink, he used to say, you're done for.

It was true, better to grumble and get on with it. Fight them, and they'd smash you.

Alyoshka lowered his face into his hands without saying a word. He was praying.

Shukhov ate his bread almost to the end, keeping back, however, a little bare crust – a semicircular bit from the top of the loaf. You could not clean out the porridge from your bowl as effectively with any spoon as you could with a piece of bread. This small crust he wrapped up again in the white cloth in preparation for his dinner, shoved the cloth into the inside pocket of his jacket, buttoned himself up against the cold and began to get ready for work – to which let them send him now,

47

although he'd prefer it if they'd wait a bit longer.

Gang 38 got up and dispersed – some to the cement-mixer, some to fetch water, some to the reinforcement meshes.

But neither Tyurin nor his second-in-command, Pavlo, had come back to the gang. And although Gang 104 had been sitting down for scarcely twenty minutes, and the working day – shortened in winter – went on until 6.00 o'clock, they still felt that they had had splendid luck, as if evening was not so far off.

"Well, it's been a long time since we had a snow-storm," sighed Kilgas, a red-faced, plump Latvian. "The whole winter – and not a snow-storm yet! What sort of winter's this!"

"Yes ... snow-storms ... snow-storms ..." sighed the members of the gang.

When there was a snow-storm in that locality, then nobody went out to work: they were frightened to let the prisoners leave the barracks. If you didn't fix a rope between the barracks and the mess-hall, you could get lost. If a prisoner froze to death in the snow? The dogs could eat him for all they cared. But if a prisoner tried to escape? There had been occasions. During a storm, the snow was as fine as it could be, but in the drifts it got packed down. Prisoners had managed to get away over these drifts when they were higher than the wire – not far, it is true.

When you thought about it, a snow-storm was no use to anyone. The prisoners had to stay in under lock and key; the coal never arrived on time, and the warmth was blown out of the barracks; no flour was delivered to the camp – so there was no bread; things went all wrong in the cook-house. And however long the snow-storm lasted – three days or a week – these days were reckoned as lost days, which had to be recovered by work on the same number of consecutive Sundays.

All the same, the prisoners loved snow-storms and prayed for them. Whenever the wind got up a bit, everyone would turn his face to the sky: "Come on, come on, let's have some real snow!"

But because the wind came across the ground, a real storm did not often brew up.

Someone tried to creep up to Gang 38's stove, but he was sent packing.

Then Tyurin came into the room. He looked gloomy. The members of the gang realised that they were going to have to get down to work, and quickly.

"So," said Tyurin, looking round. "Everybody in Gang 104 here?"

And not bothering to confirm it or to count, because none of Tyurin's gang could have gone anywhere, he quickly began to give them their orders. He sent the two Estonians and Klevshin and Gopchik to pick up the big box for mixing mortar in from nearby and to take it to the power-station. It became clear from this that the gang had been assigned to work on the unfinished part of the power-station that they had abandoned in late autumn. Another two men were sent to the tool-shop, where Pavlo was picking up some tools. Four were ordered to clear the snow from around the power-station, the entrance to the machine-room, in the machine-room itself, and from the ladders. A further two were ordered to get the stove in the machine-room going – and to get some coal, and some boards to chop up. Another was to convey some cement there on a sledge. Two were to carry water, two sand, and yet another to sweep the snow off the sand and break it up with a crowbar.

And after all this, there remained only Shukhov and Kilgas to be given jobs to – the two best workers in the gang. Calling them over to him, the gang-leader said:

"Now, boys!" – he was no older than either of them, but had got into the habit of addressing them as "boys" – "After dinner, you'll be laying slag-blocks on the second-storey walls – where Gang 6 left off in the autumn. But for the moment we must heat up the
49

machine-room. There are three big windows, and the first thing to do is find some way of boarding them up. I'll give you people to help, only you must think what to board them up with. We'll be using the machine-room for mixing mortar in – and for warming ourselves. If we don't succeed in keeping warm, we'll freeze like dogs, you understand?"

Perhaps he would have gone on, but up ran Gopchik, a lad of sixteen, as pink as a sucking-pig, complaining that another gang wouldn't give him the box for mixing mortar in, were fighting about it. So Tyurin went off to sort it out.

However tough it was to get started on the working day in cold like this, the important thing was to make a beginning, just that.

Shukhov and Kilgas looked at each other. They had worked together more than once, and viewed each other as the carpenter and the mason. It was not easy to find anything in that bare snow with which to board up the windows. But Kilgas said :

"Ivan! There, where the prefabs are, I know a little place where there's a fine roll of roofing-felt. I hid it there myself. Let's go."

Although Kilgas was a Latvian, he spoke Russian like a native – there'd been a village of Old Believers near where he lived, and he had learned the language from childhood. Kilgas had only been in camps for a couple of years, but already he understood everything : if you don't bite, you don't eat. Kilgas was named Johann, but Shukhov called him Vanya.

They decided to go for the roofing-felt. But first Shukhov ran over to fetch his trowel from the part of the automobile repair-shops which was still under construction. A trowel means something to a mason if it fits his hand and is light. However, wherever you worked, there was a rule : at night you must hand back any tool you had been given in the morning. And it was in the lap of the gods what sort of tool you got the following

50

day. But Shukhov had once managed to pull the wool over the eyes of the man in the tool-shop and got hold of the best trowel. Now he had to hide it in a different place every evening, and recover it every morning he learned he was going to be laying blocks. Of course, if Gang 104 had been sent to the Socialist Community Centre today, Shukhov would have been without a trowel again. But now he pushed aside a small stone, shoved his fingers into the crack – and, there we are, he'd got it!

Shukhov and Kilgas left the automobile repair-shops and went over to the prefabs. Their breath formed thick clouds of steam. The sun was up now, but was casting no rays, as if in a fog, and around the sun itself stood, it seemed, pillars of light.

"Like pillars, eh?" Shukhov said to Kilgas with a nod.

"There's nothing to worry about pillars," rejoined Kilgas, laughing, "so long as they don't stretch barbed wire from pillar to pillar, that's what we must watch for."

Kilgas couldn't say anything without making a joke. He was liked by all the gang on account of it. And how well the other Latvians in the camp regarded him! Of course, it was true he fed himself properly, receiving two parcels a month, and he looked well on it, as if he weren't in the camp at all. In his position, you could make jokes.

Their site *was* big – it took a while to get right across it. On the way they came across the lads from Gang 82, who'd been put on to digging up holes again. The holes didn't have to be very big: half a metre by half a metre and half a metre deep, but the ground was like stone even in the summer, and now it was completely frozen, and you might as well have gnawed at it. They used picks on it – but the picks just skidded off, showering sparks, but not an atom of earth. The lads stood there, each man to his hole, looking around – but there was nowhere to warm up, and they were forbidden to leave,

51

so they would take up their picks again. It was the only way to get warm.

Shukhov recognised someone he knew among them, a fellow from Vyatka, and he advised :

"Listen, you lot, why don't you start a little fire over each of these holes, and then the ground would thaw out."

"We're not allowed to," the man from Vyatka sighed. "They won't give us any wood."

"You must find some."

Kilgas just spat.

"Now tell me, Ivan, if the authorities had any sense at all, would they send people out in this cold to peck away at the ground with picks?"

He swore a few times under his breath and was silent. You didn't talk much when it was as cold as this. They went on and came to the place where the prefab panels were buried under the snow.

Shukhov liked to work with Kilgas: the only bad thing about him was that he did not smoke and did not get any tobacco in his parcels.

Kilgas had been dead right: the two of them picked up one panel, then another – and found the roll of roofing-felt.

They pulled it out. Now – how would they carry it? It didn't matter being noticed from a watch-tower: the guards' only worry was whether the prisoners escaped – inside the site they could chop up all the panels they wanted as far as the guards were concerned. And if a warder came across you, that didn't matter either: he'd be looking around himself for anything that would be useful to him. And the prisoners and the gang-leaders didn't give a damn for those prefabs. The only people who'd mind were a work-superintendant, a foreman who was also a prisoner and that spindleshanks Shkuropatenko. Shkuropatenko was a nobody, simply a prisoner who'd been given the job of guarding the prefabs against the prisoners' pinching them. It was this

Shkuropatenko who was most likely to catch them on the open ground.

"Look, Vanya, we mustn't carry it flat," Shukhov said. "Let's take it up on end with our arms round it, and take it slowly, shielding it with ourselves. At a distance, they won't know what it is."

Shukhov's idea was good. The roll wasn't easy to carry, so they didn't pick it up but squeezed it between themselves like a third man, and set off. From the side all you could see was two men walking close together.

"But later, when the superintendant sees this felt on the windows, he'll guess everything," Shukhov said.

"What's that to do with us?" Kilgas answered. "We can say it was there already when we got to the power-station, and should we pull it down?"

That was true.

Shukhov's fingers were numb with cold in his worn mittens; he'd completely lost all sensation in them. His left boot was holding out: that was the main thing – your felt boots. His hands would warm up when he began to work.

They crossed the untrodden snow and came to a sledge track from the tool-shop to the power-station. The cement had obviously been taken along already.

The power-station stood on a rise at the edge of the site. Nobody had been there for a long time, and all the approaches to it were covered with virgin snow. The sledge track, the new path and the deep footprints of the men in Gang 104 stood out the more clearly. And the men were already clearing away the snow from around the power-station with wooden shovels, making a way for the lorries.

It would have been good if the hoist in the power-station had been working, but the motor had burned out, and it seemed that it had not been repaired. Which meant, once again, that they would have to carry everything – the mortar and the slag-blocks – up to the second storey themselves.

The power-station had stood there for two months, like a grey skeleton in the snow, abandoned. Now Gang 104 had arrived. And what kept their spirits going? Empty bellies pulled in by rope belts; terrible cold; no warm shelter; not a spark of fire. But Gang 104 had arrived – and life began again.

At the very entrance to the machine-room the box for mixing mortar had come apart. It was a decrepit thing, that box, and Shukhov had suspected that it wouldn't make the journey in one piece. The gang-leader swore as a matter of form, but he could see that nobody was to blame. Just then Kilgas and Shukhov appeared on the scene with the roll of roofing-felt between them. The gang-leader was delighted and immediately devised a new arrangement for work: Shukhov was to fix the stove-pipe, so that the stove would warm up more quickly; Kilgas was to repair the box for mixing mortar, the two Estonians to help him; Senka Klevshin was given an axe with which to cut long laths to nail the felt to – double thickness. Where to find the laths? The superintendant certainly wouldn't give them any wood with which to make themselves a warm shelter. The gang-leader looked around, and everybody looked around. There was one way out: to remove the boards used as hand-rails for the ladders leading to the second storey. You'd have to watch out as you climbed the ladders, or you'd be for it – but what else could be done?

It might be asked why a prisoner should work so hard for ten years in a camp. Why not just chuck it and drag your feet from morning until night, which belonged to you?

But it didn't operate like that. That's why they'd thought up the system of gangs. It was not like a gang on the outside when Ivan Ivanitch would get paid separately and Pyotr Petrovitch would get paid separately. In the camp it was so arranged that it was the members of the gangs who urged each other on, not the authorities. It was like this: either you all earned a little extra, or you all went under. You're not working properly, you swine, I'm having to go hungry because of you. So sweat, you bastard!

And if a situation like the present one cropped up, then there was all the more reason not to take things easy. Like it or not, you had to get a move on. If they hadn't made somewhere to warm up in after a couple of hours, then they'd have given up the ghost anyway.

Pavlo had brought the tools now, so you had only to take your choice. And some pipes for the stove. True, the tools wouldn't have gladdened the eyes of a tin-smith, but there was a little hammer and a small-size axe. They'd manage.

Shukhov clapped his mittened hands together, joined up the pipes and fixed the joints. He clapped his hands together again and went on fixing the pipes. (He had hidden his trowel nearby. Although among men from his own gang, he wouldn't put it past one of them to snitch it – even Kilgas.)

And then every thought but one flew out of his head, and his memories and worries evaporated. He thought only of how to arrange the pipes so that they wouldn't smoke. Gopchik was sent to get a bit of wire – hang up the pipe by the window, that was the answer.

In the corner there was another stove, a thickset one with a brick chimney. It had an iron plate on top, which grew red-hot and was used to thaw out and dry the sand. This stove had already been lit, and the captain and Fetyukov were carrying sand there in hand-barrows. You don't need brains to carry a hand-barrow. That's why the gang-leader gave this kind of work to people who had formerly been in a position of authority. Fetyukov had been a big shot in some kind of office, and had travelled around in a car.

In the early days Fetyukov had treated the captain like muck and had yelled at him. But the captain had landed him one in the teeth, and now they got on all right.

The lads bringing in the sand had sidled up to the stove, but the gang-leader warned them off.

"Watch out, or I'll tan one of you! Get the place fixed up first!"

Beat a dog once and you have only to show him the whip. The cold was ferocious, but not as ferocious as the gang-leader. The men went back to work again.

And Shukhov heard the gang-leader say softly to Pavlo:

"You stay here and keep them at it. I'll go now and settle the percentage."

More depended on the percentage than on the work itself. A clever gang-leader was one who gave his mind to the percentage. That is how they ate. If something had not been done, make it look as though it had; if the percentage had been assessed low, then get it up. To do this a gang-leader had to have brains in his head – and be cosy with the norm-checkers, who would have to be suitably persuaded.

But, come to think of it, who were these percentages for? For the camp. The camp got thousands on top from the construction people and were able to hand out bonuses to the officers – like Volkovoi, for using his whip. And you? You got an extra 200 grams of bread in the evening. 200 grams was the difference between life and death.

Two buckets of water were brought in, but they had frozen on the way. Pavlo reckoned that it was pointless to carry the water like that. Quicker to melt down the snow. They put the buckets on the stove.

Gopchik brought some new electric wire – such as electricians used.

"Ivan Denisovitch!" he said. "This wire's good for making spoons. Will you teach me how to cast a spoon?"

Ivan Denisovitch liked this Gopchik, the rascal (his own son had died young, and he had two grown-up daughters). Gopchik had been arrested for taking bread into the forest for Bendera's* followers. They had given him an adult's sentence. He was like an affectionate little calf, and he fawned on everybody. But he was artful, too: he ate the contents of his parcels on his own, sometimes during the night.

But you couldn't feed everybody, that's for sure.

They broke off some wire for the spoons and hid it in a corner. Shukhov fashioned a step-ladder out of a couple of planks, and sent Gopchik up it to hang the stove-pipe. Gopchik, as agile as a squirrel, clambered along the beams, banged in a nail, threw the wire over and fixed it to support the pipe. Shukhov, however, was not idle, and he used one knee to make another bend in the top of the pipe. It was not so windy today, but it might be tomorrow – and this would stop the pipe smoking. One had to understand, the stove was for them – for them.

Senka Klevshin had made the long laths now. Gopchik was put to nailing these up as well. He climbed up, the little devil, and shouted down to the men below.

The sun had risen higher now, dispersing the haze, and those pillars Shukhov had remarked on had gone – there was a reddish glow inside the room. Now they had got the stove going with stolen wood. Much more cheerful!

"Only cows get warmed by the sun in January," Shukhov said.

Kilgas finished nailing together the box for mixing mortar, gave it one last tap, and shouted:

"Listen, Pavlo, I won't take less than 100 roubles from the gang-leader for this job!"

Pavlo laughed:

"You'll get 100 grams."

"The public prosecutor will make up the difference!" Gopchik shouted from above.

* A Soviet General who collaborated with the Germans in World War II.

"Hold it, hold it!" Shukhov cried. (They were cutting the roofing-felt wrong.)

He showed them how to do it.

The men were sidling up to the iron stove, but Pavlo drove them off. He gave some helpers to Kilgas and ordered them to make hods for the mortar to be carried to the second storey. He put another pair of men onto carrying sand. He sent others up to clear the scaffolding and the place where the blocks would be laid of snow – and another inside to throw the hot sand from the stove into the box for mixing mortar.

Outside a motor could be heard turning over – they were beginning to deliver the blocks; the lorry had arrived. Pavlo ran out and waved his hands to show them where to unload the blocks.

They put up one strip of roofing-felt, then the second. But what protection do you get from roofing-felt? It was paper, just paper. Nevertheless, it made a solid wall of a kind. And it was darker inside – so the stove looked brighter.

Alyoshka brought in some coal. Some shouted: "Pour it on!" others: "No, don't, we'll get warmer with wood!" He just stood there, not knowing whom to obey.

Fetyukov found a place near the stove and put his felt boots right up to the fire, the idiot. The captain lifted him up by the scruff of the neck and jostled him over to the barrows:

"Go and get sand, you bastard!"

The captain – he looked upon work in the camp as service in the navy: if you were told to do something, you did it. He had grown very emaciated in the last month, but he was holding up.

Before too long, all three windows were covered with roofing-felt. Light only came through the doors now. And with it the cold, too. Pavlo ordered the upper half of the doorway to be boarded up, leaving the lower half free – enough to let the men, heads bent, get through.

Meanwhile three lorries had driven up and discarded their loads of blocks. The problem now was to get them up to the second storey without the use of a hoist.

"Masons! Let's go up and look round!" Pavlo called.

Laying blocks was a job worthy of respect. Shukhov and Kilgas went up with Pavlo. The ladder was in any case narrow, but now that Senka had torn away the hand-rails, you had to stick close to the wall if you didn't want to fall off. And still worse – the snow had frozen to the steps, and had rounded them so that you couldn't get a grip for your feet. How were they going to get the mortar up?

They looked around to see where on the walls to lay blocks – the men were shovelling away the snow already. Here was the place. They'd have to take an axe to the ice on the old blocks and then sweep them clean.

They figured how to get the blocks up. They looked down. They decided it would be a mistake to use the ladder, better to have four men on the ground to throw the blocks to that scaffolding there, then another two to throw them to the second storey, and two more men to carry them on from there – that would be quicker than the ladder.

The wind wasn't strong up there, but you could feel it. It would penetrate all right when they began to lay. If they got behind the wall that had been started on, they'd be protected to some extent, however – not much, but it would be slightly warmer.

Shukhov looked up at the sky and gasped: it was quite clear, and the sun showed it was almost dinner-time. Wonder of wonders, how time went by when you were working! Shukhov had noticed that many times: the days rolled by in the camp – before you could say "knife"! But your sentence – that didn't seem to go by, the end never seemed to be in sight.

They went down and there found that everyone had settled round the stove, except for the captain and Fetyukov who were still carrying sand. Pavlo blew up, and immediately drove eight of the men out to get blocks, ordered two to start pouring cement into the box and stirring in the sand, another to fetch water, another to fetch coal.

"Come on, lads, we must finish these hods," Kilgas said to those who had been working with him.

"Shall I help them?" Shukhov asked Pavlo.

"Yes," Pavlo said and nodded.

They brought up a can in which to melt snow for the mortar. They heard from somebody that it was already noon.

"That's right," said Shukhov. "The sun is directly overhead."

"If it's overhead," retorted the captain, "that means it's not noon, but one o'clock."

"How so?" questioned Shukhov. "Any old man knows that the sun's at its highest when it's time for dinner."

"Any old man – maybe!" snapped the captain. "But since then a decree has been issued that the sun is at its highest at one o'clock."

"Who issued the decree?"

"The Soviet Government!"

The captain went out with a barrow. Shukhov wasn't going to argue with him in any case. Surely the sun wasn't subject to their decrees as well?

There was more banging and hammering, and they knocked together four hods.

"O.K., sit down and warm yourselves," Pavlo said to the two masons. "And you, Senka, you'll be laying blocks with them after dinner, too. Sit down!"

And now they sat by the stove quite lawfully. They couldn't start laying before dinner in any case, and if they started carrying the mortar up, it would freeze.

The coal was beginning to grow red-hot, and was now

throwing out a regular heat. But it only reached you near the stove, and in the rest of the room, it was as cold as always.

They took off their mittens, and all four of them held their hands near the stove.

It was important never to do one thing – put your feet near the flames if you were wearing boots. If they were leather, then the leather cracked, and if they were felt boots, they got damp and began to steam, and you didn't feel any warmer – and if you put them close to the fire, they burned. Then you had to walk around until spring with a hole in them, you wouldn't get any others.

"What's Shukhov got to worry about?" Kilgas joked. "Shukhov's got one foot at home already."

"Yes, the bare one," said someone. They laughed. (Shukhov had taken off his left boot – the one needing to be repaired – and was warming his foot-cloths.)

"Shukhov's sentence is almost over."

They'd given Kilgas twenty-five years. Earlier, things had been better: ten years without exception to everybody. But since '49, it had gone up: twenty-five years, irrespective. One could live through ten years – but who could get out alive after twenty-five?

Shukhov liked it that everybody pointed at him – him, the one whose sentence was almost over. But he did not really believe in it. Remember the prisoners whose sentences should have finished during the war – all that lot had been retained until '46 "pending special instructions". And then those with three-year sentences had found themselves with another five to serve. The law can be turned any way you want. You served your ten years, and perhaps they'd give you another ten. Or they'd exile you.

But there were times when you thought about it – and your spirits soared: your sentence was coming to an end, the string was running out ... God, to go out on your own two legs – free ...?

But it wasn't done for an old camp hand to talk out loud about it. Shukhov said to Kilgas:

"Don't you concern yourself about those twenty-five years. Who knows whether you'll be here for the full twenty-five? That I have done eight full years I know for sure."

So you went on living like this with your face on the ground, and there was no time to be thinking how you got in and how you'd get out.

According to his papers, Shukhov had been sentenced for high treason. He had given evidence against himself to the effect that he had surrendered to the enemy, intending to betray his country, had returned from captivity in order to carry out instructions given by the Germans. Just what these instructions were, neither Shukhov nor the interrogator were able to say. So they left it like that – "instructions".

It was a simple calculation for Shukhov: if he didn't sign, he'd be shot; if he did, he would live on for a while. He signed.

This is what happened: in February '42, their whole army had been encircled on the North-West Front. They didn't send in any provisions by air; there weren't any aeroplanes. Things reached such a pitch that they were cutting the hooves off dead horses – which they would then soften by soaking in water and eat. They had no ammunition. So the Germans hunted them down a few at a time and took them prisoner. Shukhov was in one such group, was held in captivity for a couple of days there in the forest. Then five of them managed to escape. They crept through the forest and marshes and, by a miracle, reached their own lines. A machine-gunner killed two of them on the spot, and a third died of his wounds – so two of them got through. If they'd had any sense, they would have said that they'd been wandering around in the forest, and everything would have been all right. But they told the truth: they had escaped from the Germans. Escaped, you fuckers! If the five of them had got back, their statements would have coincided, and maybe they would have been believed, but only two: not a hope. The bastards had fixed the whole escape story!

Deaf as he was, Senka Klevshin heard that they were talking about escaping from the Germans, and said loudly:

"I escaped three times, and three times they got me."

Senka, who had suffered so much, was mostly silent: he couldn't hear what people said and did not involve himself in their conversations. They didn't know much about him, only that he'd been in Buchenwald and had been in the underground organisation there, smuggling in arms for an uprising. The Germans had hung him up with his hands tied behind his back and beaten him with rods.

"You've been in for eight years, Ivan – but what kind of camps?" Kilgas asked. "You were in regular camps, where you could sleep with women. You didn't have to wear numbers. But what about eight years in a penal camp? Nobody gets through that alive!"

"Women . . . logs, not women!"

Shukhov stared into the stove and remembered his seven years in the North. The way he'd hauled logs for three years – for making crates and sleepers. The camp-fire had danced just like this in the forest camp – not during the day of course, but when they worked at night. The Commandant's rule was that if a gang failed to do its daily quota, then it stayed in the forest until it had done, night or no night.

They would get back to the camp at about midnight and would have to go out into the forest again the following morning.

"No, no, brothers . . . it's a more peaceful life here, believe me," he lisped through his missing teeth. "Here it's regular: if you've finished, or you haven't finished – you go back to camp at the end of the day. And a guarantee here of a hundred grams more bread than up there. Here one can live. It may be a "special" camp, but so what? Does it worry you to wear numbers? Numbers don't weigh anything."

"More peaceful!" Fetyukov hissed. (It was nearly time for the dinner-break, and everyone had moved up around the stove.) "When you can get your throat cut in your bed! More peaceful!"

"Only squealers get their throats cut!" Pavlo raised a menacing finger at Fetyukov.

It was true, something new had started at the camp. Two well-known squealers had been found dead in their bunks before reveille. And not long after the same thing had happened to an innocent prisoner – they must have mistaken the bunk. And one of the squealers had run off to the Chief Prison Officer, and they'd given him refuge there in the stone-walled prison block.

It was astonishing . . . that sort of thing did not occur in ordinary camps. Nor here until recently . . .

Suddenly the hooter went. It never achieved full force first thing, but sounded rather hoarse, as if clearing its throat.

Half way through! Down tools! The dinner-break!

Oh, they'd delayed things! They should have gone to the mess-hall long ago to get in the queue. There were eleven gangs on the site, and no more than two could fit into the mess-hall at one time.

The gang-leader hadn't come back. Pavlo looked round rapidly and then decided:

"Shukhov and Gopchik – come with me! Kilgas, when Gopchik gets back to you, send the rest of the gang over immediately!"

Their places at the stove were taken at once, and the way the men surrounded it, it was if it were a woman they were embracing.

"That's it!" they shouted. "Let's have a smoke."

And they looked at each other to see who would light up. Nobody did – either they had no tobacco or they were holding it back because they didn't want anybody to see that they had.

Shukhov went out with Pavlo; and Gopchik bounced after them.

"It's warmer," Shukhov observed when they were outside. No more than −18. It'll be good for laying the blocks."

They glanced at the blocks – many of them had already been thrown up to the scaffolding, and a number had been taken on to the second storey.

Shukhov, screwing up his eyes against the sun, confirmed its decreed position according to the captain.

Outside, where there was nothing to interrupt the wind, it was strong and sharp. Don't forget, it was saying, remember that this is January.

The cook-house on the site was a small shack made of boards around a stove – to cover the cracks, they'd fixed some rusty metal sheets. Inside, the shack was separated into a kitchen and a place to eat. Neither area had a proper floor. The earth had been trampled down by the men's feet, and was full of holes and ridges. And the kitchen – a square stove with a cauldron on top.

The kitchen was run by two men – a cook and a sanitary inspector. When he left the camp in the morning, the cook received some groats from the main camp kitchen – fifty grams per head or a kilogram per gang, less than sixteen kilograms for all the men working on the site. The cook wasn't going to carry that himself over three kilometers, so he had an assistant to carry it for him: better to give the assistant an extra portion at the expense of the prisoners than break his own back. There was water to be carried, too, and wood with which to light the stove – again, things the cook didn't relish, so more assistants and more extra portions at the prisoners' expense. It's easy to be generous with what does not belong to you. It was established that you had to eat without leaving the mess-hall; so the bowls had to be brought from the camp (you couldn't leave them on the site overnight since they would get stolen by the free workers) – about fifty bowls were so conveyed, not more, and they were quickly washed for use by the next man. (Of course, the man who carried the bowls also got an extra portion.) To prevent the bowls being taken out of the mess-hall, they posted a man on the door. But however watchful he was, people took them out all the same – either by talking their way through or nipping by when he wasn't looking. So yet another person had to go round the site, the whole site, collecting dirty bowls and taking them back to the kitchen. An extra portion for him, too, naturally.

The only thing the cook did was put the groats and the salt into the cauldron, sharing the fat between himself and the cauldron (good fat never got as far as the prisoners, only the bad stuff – which went into the cauldron. But the prisoners couldn't afford to mind whether the fat given out by the stores was bad). The cook also stirred the porridge when it was just about ready. The sanitary inspector didn't do as much: he sat and watched. But when the porridge was ready, then he ate to capacity – as did the cook. Then the gang-leader of the day arrived – they took it in turns, the gang-leaders – to sample the stuff to see whether it was good enough for the men to eat. He got a double portion.

The hooter sounded. The gang-leaders at once formed a queue, and the cook handed them bowls through a little hatch, and in the bottom of each bowl lay some of the porridge – whether your fair share or not you didn't ask or seek to assess by the weight: if you opened your mouth at all, you'd get it in the neck.

The wind whistled over the bare steppe – in summer, a hot, dry wind, in winter, a freezing one. Nothing would ever grow on that steppe, still less behind four rows of barbed wire. As far as they were concerned, the only place where bread came from was the bread-store, and oats from the oats-store. And however much you broke your back working, or lay back in despair, you'd cull no food from that ground – you got no more than was issued to you by the Commandant. Ana you didn't get that either – what with the cooks and their assistants and helpers. You got short measure all the way – on the site, in the camp, even earlier – in the store-rooms. And you never saw any of those fiddlers taking up a pick. No, you did the work, and took what you were given. And didn't linger round the hatch.

You feathered your own nest as best you could.

Pavlo, Shukhov and Gopchik entered the mess-hall – there, the prisoners stood so close to one another that you couldn't see the tables and benches for their backs. Some were eating sitting down, but mostly they stood. Gang 82, who'd spent the morning digging those holes without any kind of protection – they'd been the first to get seats after the hooter had gone. And now that they'd finished eating, they weren't going – where else could they get any warmth? The others were swearing at them, but it was as much use as swearing at a blank wall – it was so much more pleasant here than in the cold.

Pavlo and Shukhov elbowed their way through. They had come at a good time: one gang had been served, another was waiting in turn, and the seconds-in-command of the gangs were standing by the hatch. They were next.

"Bowls! Bowls!" the cook shouted through the hatch, and they were pushed through to him from the other side. In addition, Shukhov collected up some bowls and pushed them through – not to earn himself an extra portion, but the more quickly to get his ration.

Behind the partition some helpers were already washing the bowls – to get something extra for themselves.

The gang second-in-command in front of Pavlo was beginning to get the food for his gang – and Pavlo shouted across the heads:

"Gopchik!"

"Here!" came a squeaky little voice from the door, like a young goat.

"Call the gang!"

Gopchik ran off.

The main thing was that the porridge today was good – oatmeal, the best sort. They didn't get it often. As a rule, it was magara twice a day, or meal. Oatmeal was good, and filling.

How many times had Shukhov fed oats to horses in his youth! He never thought he'd be craving with his whole soul for a handful of just such oats!

"Bowls! Bowls!" they cried through the hatch.

Gang 104's turn was approaching. The gang second-in-command ahead got his double ration and moved away from the hatch.

This was also at the expense of the other prisoners – but nobody questioned it. Every gang-leader received such an extra portion, and he either ate it himself or gave it to his second-in-command. Tyurin gave his to Pavlo.

Now Shukhov had to squeeze himself in behind a table – chase away a couple of men who had finished but not left, politely ask another to leave, and clear a space on the table for twelve bowls pushed up together, on top of which he would put another six and then another two. Then he would take the bowls from Pavlo, repeating out loud the number he took and keeping an eye out that nobody else grabbed a bowl from the table – or jostled him into upsetting one. On either side of him people were either getting up from the bench, sitting down or eating. It was essential to keep a sharp eye open – were they eating from their own bowls, or had they got hold of those for Gang 104?

"Two! Four! Six!" the cook counted behind the hatch. He gave out the bowls two at a time. It was easier for him that way, and he didn't lose count.

"Two, four, six," Pavlo repeated softly to him through the hatch. And immediately he passed the bowls in pairs to Shukhov, who placed them on the table. Shukhov did not repeat the count out loud, but his eye was keener than anybody's.

"Eight, ten."

Why hadn't Gopchik brought in the gang?

"Twelve, fourteen . . ." went the count.

Then they ran out of bowls in the kitchen. Beyond Pavlo's head and shoulders, Shukhov saw the hands of the cook putting two bowls down onto the hatch; the hands held on to the bowls, as if the cook were contemplating something. Perhaps he had turned to curse the dishwashers. Then another pile of bowls was pushed through the hatch. He released his hands from the two bowls and pushed the other pile back.

Shukhov left the pile of bowls he had so far assembled on the table, jumped over the bench, seized both the bowls, and, not so much for the cook as for Pavlo, repeated in a not very loud voice:

"Fourteen."

"Stop! Where are you taking those?" the cook shouted.

"They're ours, they're ours!" Pavlo assured him.

"They may be yours, but don't make me lose count!"

"Fourteen," Pavlo said, shrugging his shoulders. He himself would not have whipped the extra bowls; as a second-in-command, he had to maintain his authority. But he had simply repeated what Shukhov said, and he could always blame it on him.

"I'd already said fourteen!" the cook raged.

"Of course you said it, but you didn't pass them out, you kept your hands on them!" Shukhov shouted. "Go and count them if you don't believe me! They are all there, on the table!"

While Shukhov was shouting at the cook, he noticed that the two Estonians, as close to each other as always, were pushing their way up to him, and he shoved the bowls into their hands as they passed. Then he hurriedly turned back to the table to establish that all the bowls were in place, and that nobody sitting nearby had pinched any – although they could easily have done so.

The cook's red face showed itself halfway through the hatch.

"Where are those bowls?" he asked threateningly.

"Here we are!" cried Shukhov. "Get along there, you fucker, he can't see!" He pushed somebody aside. "Here we are – two bowls!" He picked up two bowls from the top of the pile of bowls on the table. "And there are three rows of four left, correct? Count them!"

"But hasn't your gang arrived?" The cook looked suspiciously round the small area of the mess-hall visible to him through the hatch – itself narrow and small so as to prevent people looking in from the mess-hall to see how much there was left in the cauldron.

"No, they're not here yet," Pavlo said, shaking his head.

"Then why the hell are you taking bowls if your gang isn't there yet?" he shouted furiously.

"Here they are, they're coming!" Shukhov shouted.

Everybody could hear the yelling of the captain in the doorway – as if he were on his bridge.

"Why are you all crowding round? If you've eaten, get out. Give way for other people!"

The cook grumbled something else, straightened himself up, and his hands showed again in the hatch.

"Sixteen, eighteen . . ."

Then he poured out the last bowl, a double portion:

"Twenty-three. That's it! Next!"

The members of the gang began to push their way over to the table, and Pavlo handed them their bowls – some over the heads of prisoners seated at a second table.

In the summer five men could sit at one bench, but now they were so bulkily dressed that scarcely four could squeeze in, and it wasn't easy for them to move their spoons.

Reckoning that, of the two bowls he had contrived

to swipe, one of them would be his, Shukhov lost no time in getting down to eat. He raised his right knee to his stomach, pulled the spoon marked "Ust-Izhma, 1944" from his boot, took off his cap, tucked it under his left arm and stirred his porridge round the edge of the bowl with his spoon.

This was the moment when one gave everything to the act of eating – taking the porridge from the meagre contents at the bottom of the bowl, putting it resolutely into one's mouth, and rolling it around with one's tongue. But Shukhov had to hurry, so that Pavlo could see that he had already finished and offer him a second bowl. And there was Fetyukov, who had come in together with the Estonians, who had seen everything with the two extra bowls, and who was now eating, standing directly opposite Pavlo, looking at the four extra portions which had accrued to the gang. He was seeking to show Pavlo that he should get, if not a whole extra portion, at least a half-portion.

The young, swarthy Pavlo, however, went on eating quite calmly, and there was nothing on his face to indicate that he had noticed that anyone was standing in front of him, or that he had remembered the extra portions at all.

Shukhov finished his bowl of porridge. Because he had let his belly know of the possibility of another portion, it did not feel satisfied with the one, as it usually did with oatmeal. He reached into his inside pocket, took the unfrozen, semi-circular piece of crust from the clean cloth, and with it carefully began to wipe all that remained of the oatmeal porridge at the bottom of the bowl and around the edges. When there was enough on the crust, he licked it clean and then went through the same process again. Finally the bowl was as clean as if it had been washed, only not as shiny. He handed the bowl over his shoulder to one of the people collecting bowls, and continued to sit there without putting his cap back on.

71

Although Shukhov had swiped the extra bowls, it was not his business to dispose of them – but the second-in-command's.

Pavlo delayed things a little further, while he finished his own bowl, but he didn't lick it clean, merely passed his tongue over his spoon, put it away and crossed himself. Then he lightly touched – there was no room to push them – two of the four bowls, in that way giving them to Shukhov.

"Ivan Denisovitch, take one for yourself and give the other to Tsesar."

Shukhov had remembered that one of the bowls would have to be taken to Tsesar in the office (Tsesar would never have lowered himself to go to the mess-hall, either here or in the camp, to get it) – he had remembered all right, but when Pavlo touched the two bowls at the same time, Shukhov's heart had contracted: had Pavlo given him both the extra bowls? And now his heart returned to normal.

And now he inclined himself over his lawful prize and began to eat very deliberately, not feeling it when members of the new gang which had arrived jostled him in the back. The only thing that bothered him was that Fetyukov might get the other bowl. Fetyukov was a master at cadging, but he never had the courage to pinch anything himself.

Captain Buinovsky sat near them at the table. He had finished his porridge some time ago, and did not know that the gang had any extra portions, and he did not look around to see how many bowls Pavlo had still to dispose of. He was simply taking it easy, warming up, but he did not have the strength to stand up and go out into the cold again, or to the shelter against the cold which they had made at the power-station – which was really no shelter at all. So now he was occupying a place in the mess-hall he had no entitlement to, and was a hindrance to the members of the gangs which were arriving – just like those whom, five minutes be-

72

fore, he had been driving out with his authoritarian voice. He had not been long in the camp and was unused to labouring. Such moments as these (he did not know this) were especially important to him, converting him from a powerful, brisk naval officer into a slow-moving, watchful prisoner, and it was only that slow-moving quality which would give him the capacity to survive the twenty-five years' imprisonment he had been sentenced to.

People were already shouting at him and pushing him in the back to get him to give up his place.

Pavlo said:

"Hey, captain! Captain!"

Buinovsky started, as if roused from sleep, and looked round.

Pavlo handed him the porridge, not asking him whether he wanted it or not.

Buinovsky's eyebrows shot up, and his eyes regarded the porridge as if it were some unseen miracle.

"Take it, take it," Pavlo encouraged him and, picking up the last bowl for the gang-leader, he went out.

A guilty smile passed over the captain's chapped lips – the lips of him who had sailed round Europe and through the Arctic Ocean. And he bent forward, happily, over the meagrely filled bowl of thin oatmeal porridge, cooked without fat – only oats and water.

Fetyukov looked maliciously at Shukhov, at the captain, and left.

And Shukhov felt that it had been right for the captain to get the extra bowl. As time went by, the captain would learn to cope, but for the moment he did not know how.

Shukhov still had one faint hope – that Tsesar would give him his bowl of porridge. But why should he, when he hadn't received a parcel for two weeks now?

Having scraped the bottom and edge of the bowl with the crust of bread and having licked the crust clean as before, Shukhov finally ate the crust itself. Then he picked up Tsesar's by now cold porridge and went out.

"For someone in the office!" he said to the cook's assistant at the door, who tried to stop him going through with a bowl.

The office was a wooden hut near the guard-room. Even now, as in the morning, smoke was pouring out of the chimney. An orderly kept the stove going, and acted as a messenger as well, picking up a bit on the side from time to time. The office never went short of wood.

The outer door creaked as Shukhov opened it – and then the other door, caulked with oakum – and, bringing with him a cloud of frosty steam, he went in, rapidly closing the door behind him (so that they wouldn't shout at him: "Hey, you, you bastard, shut the door!")

The heat in the office was like in the bath-house, it seemed to him. The sun, shining through the melting frost on the windows, played on the wall opposite not angrily as it did on top of the power-station, but cheerfully. And the smoke from Tsesar's pipe drifted across the broad sunbeam like incense in church. And the stove glowed red-hot, it had been so well fed – the brutes! The pipes were red-hot, too.

In such warmth, you had only to sit down for a moment, and you'd be fast asleep.

There were two rooms in the office. The second, the Chief Work-Superintendant's, had its door half-open, and from it thundered the voice of its occupant:

"We've been spending too much on labour, and we've been spending too much on building materials. The prisoners have been chopping up expensive boards, not to speak of prefab panels, and burning them in their shelters, and you notice nothing. And the other day they were unloading cement near the stores in a strong wind, and then carrying it in barrows for up to ten yards, with the result that the whole area around the stores was ankle-deep in cement, and the prisoners covered with the stuff. What a waste!"

The Chief Work-Superintendant must have been having a conference – with the foremen.

The orderly was sitting dreamily on a stool in the corner by the entrance. Beyond was Shkuropatenko, B–219, looking like a bent pole, staring wall-eyed through the window, even now looking to see if anybody tried to get away with his prefabs. The old fool had been taken for a ride over the roofing-felt.

Two bookkeepers – also prisoners – were toasting bread at the stove. They'd fixed up a wire grill to prevent it burning.

Tsesar was smoking his pipe, sprawled in his chair by a table. He had his back to Shukhov and couldn't see him.

Opposite him at the table sat X–123, a scrawny old man who had served twenty years. He was eating porridge.

"No, old chap," Tsesar was saying in a gentle, tolerant way, "objectively speaking, one must admit that Eisenstein was a genius. 'Ivan the Terrible' – is not that a work of genius? The dance of the masked *oprichniki*! The scene in the cathedral!"

"Affected!" said X–123 angrily, holding his spoon in front of his mouth. "So much art is no art at all. Pepper and poppy-seed instead of good, honest bread! And then the political thesis is vile – the justification of a one-man tyranny. A mockery of the memory of three generations of the Russian intelligentsia!" (He ate his porridge with a mouth that seemed not to be able to taste, it was wasted on him).

"But what other treatment would have been permitted ... ?"

"Ugh! Permitted! Then do not speak of him as a genius! Call him a toady, say that he carried out orders like a dog! A genius does not adapt his treatment to the taste of tyrants!"

"Hm, hm," Shukhov cleared his throat, hesitant to interrupt this cultured conversation. But he couldn't just go on standing there.

75

Tsesar turned, held out his hand for the bowl, not looking at Shukhov – as if the porridge itself had appeared from thin air – and then carried on:

"But listen, art – art isn't a question of *what*, but of *how*".

X–123 beat the table repeatedly with the edge of his hand.

"No, no, no! To hell with your 'how' if it doesn't arouse any decent feelings in me!"

Shukhov stood there for as long as it was fitting for a man to stand who had just delivered some porridge. He waited, feeling that Tsesar might give him a smoke. But Tsesar had completely forgotten that he was standing there, behind him.

So, turning, Shukhov left quietly.

It wasn't too cold outside. The block laying should go quite well.

As he walked along the path, Shukhov saw a piece of metal lying in the snow – it was off a hacksaw blade. Although he could envisage no specific use for such a piece ... but you never knew what you might need in the future, and he picked it up and put it into his knee-pocket. He'd hide it at the power-station. A thrifty man is better than a rich one.

Reaching the power-station, before anything else he recovered his hidden trowel and pushed it behind his rope belt. Then he ducked into the machine-room.

There, after the sun, it seemed quite dark and not as warm as it had been outside. Damper somehow.

The men were gathered about the round stove which Shukhov had fixed up, and the stove where, steaming, the sand was being dried. Those with no place by either of the stoves sat on the edge of the box for mixing mortar. The gang-leader sat right by the stove, finishing his porridge, which Pavlo had heated for him on the stove.

The lads were whispering among themselves. They were very cheerful. They told Ivan Denisovitch in quiet voices that the gang-leader had managed to get a good

76

percentage. He had come back in a good mood.

What sort of work he'd said they'd been doing – and where – that was his, the gang-leader's affair. What, in fact, had they done today until dinner? Nothing. Fixing up the stove and making a shelter didn't count as work: that was for themselves, not for the good of production. But something would have to be written in the work-report. Perhaps Tsesar would help the gang-leader to fiddle things – the gang-leader was respectful to Tsesar, and that must indicate something.

"A good percentage" – that meant that they would now get good bread rations for five days. Well, maybe not five, but four: the authorities would do the dirty on one day out of five for sure, would put the whole camp on a guaranteed minimum – to apply equally to the good as to the bad. So that nobody should feel offended, equal rations for all! And the camp would be saving at the expense of the prisoners' bellies. Well, a prisoner's belly can put up with anything: get through today somehow, and eat tomorrow. It was with that dream that they lay down to sleep in the camp on the day of a guaranteed minimum.

Thinking about it – it was five days' work for four days' food.

The gang was quiet. Those who could, were smoking unobtrusively. They huddled together in the dark and looked at the fire. Like one big family. It was like a family, the team. They listened to the gang-leader as he recounted a story to two or three of them by the stove. He never wasted his words, and if he allowed himself to talk, then it meant that he was in good spirits.

He also had never learned to eat with his cap on, Andrei Prokofyevitch; and without it, he looked old. His head was closely shaven – like all the prisoners' – but in the light of the stove you could see how many grey hairs he had.

"... I was frightened enough in front of the battalion commander, but here I was before the regimental commander! 'Private of the Red Army at your disposal...' He looked at me under his thick eyebrows: 'And your name and patronymic?' I tell him. 'Year of birth?' I tell him. It was 1930 then, and I was twenty-two, a kid. 'Well, Tyurin, who are you serving?' 'I serve the working people.' At which he blew up, and banged both his hands on the table. 'You serve the working people, but who are you, you bastard?' Inside I was raging, but I kept control. 'Machine-gunner, first class. Distinction in military and political...' 'First class – what do you mean, you swine? Your father's a kulak. Look, these papers are from Kamen! Your father's a kulak, and you've been hiding. They've been looking for you for two years.' I went pale and kept silent. I hadn't written home for a year in order that they wouldn't catch up with me. I didn't know whether they were still alive – and they knew nothing about me. 'What about your conscience!' he shouted – all four shoulder straps shaking with his anger – 'Deceiving the Workers' and the Peasants' Government?' I thought he was going to beat me. But he didn't. He signed an order to have me booted out of the gates within six hours... And it was November. They stripped me of my winter uniform and gave me a summer one – third hand, it must have been – and a short greatcoat. I didn't know that I could have kept my winter uniform, and told them to go to hell... And they sent me off with a stinking reference: 'Discharged from the ranks ... as the son of a kulak.' Fat chance of picking up a job with that! It was a four days' train journey to get home – and they didn't give me a free pass, or anything to eat even for a single day. I got dinner there for the last time, and then they chucked me out of the garrison.

"By the way, in '38, at the Kotlas transit centre, I met my old platoon commander – they'd given him ten years. I learned from him that both the regimental commander and the commissar had been shot in '37. Whether they were proletarian or kulak, whether they had a conscience or not ... I crossed myself and said: 'So, Creator, You are up there in heaven after all. You have plenty of patience, but when You strike, You really do'."

After the two bowls of porridge, Shukhov longed desperately to smoke. And presupposing that he could buy from the Latvian in Barracks 7 those two jars of home-grown tobacco and then square things, Shukhov said quietly to the Estonian fisherman:

"Listen, Eino, lend me enough for one cigarette until tomorrow. You know I won't let you down."

Eino looked Shukhov straight in the eye, and then, not hurrying, turned towards his "brother". They shared everything, and wouldn't dispose of a shred of tobacco without the other knowing. They muttered something together, and Eino reached for his pouch sewn with pink cord. Out of the pouch he took a pinch of factory-made tobacco, placed it in Shukhov's hand, measured it and then added a little more. Enough for a single smoke, no more.

Shukhov had some newspaper. He tore a piece off, rolled a cigarette, picked up a coal which had rolled between the gang-leader's legs, and lit it – and dragged and dragged! And a heady feeling pervaded the whole of his body, as if the effect of the cigarette were reaching his legs as well as his head.

As soon as he began to smoke, he spotted a pair of green eyes sparkling at him across the hut: Fetyukov's. He might have softened and given the jackal a pull, but Shukhov had seen him score one success at his cadging game already today. Better to leave something for Senka Klevshin. He wasn't able to hear the gang-leader recounting his story, and had just sat there, poor wretch, in front of the stove with his head on one side.

The gang-leader's pock-marked face was lit by the flames from the stove. He continued his story without self-pity, as if he were talking about somebody else:

"The odds and ends I had, such as they were, I sold

to a dealer for a quarter of their value, and I bought a couple of loaves of bread under the counter – there was rationing then. I thought I'd hop a goods' train, but they'd just brought in some tough penalties for that. And you couldn't buy tickets then, remember, even with money, let alone without it – you had to have an authorised travel voucher. You couldn't even get on the platform: there were militiamen at the barrier, and guards wandering up and down both sides of the tracks. The watery sun was setting, and the puddles were beginning to freeze over. Where could I spend the night? I climbed up a smooth brick wall, jumped down with my loaves of bread – and got into the platform lavatory. I stayed there a while – but nobody was after me. Then I came out as if I were a passenger – a soldier in transit. And there stood the Vladivostok–Moscow train. There was a rush for boiling water, and people were hitting each other on the head with their kettles. At the edge of the crowd was a girl wearing a blue blouse and carrying a large-size tea-kettle – but she was too frightened to make her way to the hot water point. Frightened to get her little feet scalded or trodden on. 'Here,' I said, 'take these loaves, and I'll get some hot water for you.' While I was filling the kettle, the train began to move. She was holding on to my loaves and crying: she did not know what to do with them; she would gladly have thrown away the kettle. 'Run!' I cried. 'Run! I'll follow you.' And off she went, with me behind her. I caught up with her and hoisted her on with one arm – and ran alongside the train myself. I – I got one foot on. The conductor didn't try to bang my fingers or push me in the chest: there were other soldiers in the carriage, and he must have taken me for one of them."

Shukhov nudged Senka in the ribs to get him to take his dog-end, poor devil. He gave it to him in its wooden holder – let him drag at it, it was all right by him. Senka, the dolt, responded like an actor – put his hand over his heart and bowed his head. But he was deaf, after all . . .

The gang-leader went on with his story:

"There were six of them in the special compartment – all girls, Leningrad students returning from a practical course. They had some splendid things to eat on their little table, their coats were hung up on hangers, and their cases had covers on them. They were going through life easy – it was the green light for them, all right . . . We talked and joked and drank tea together. They asked me which carriage I had come from. I sighed and told them the truth. 'Girls, the carriage I come from, unlike this, has death as its destination . . .'"

It was silent in the machine-room – just the stove roaring.

"After some aah-ing and ooh-ing, they conferred together – with the result that they hid me under their coats on the top berth. Hiding me like that, they got me as far as Novosibirsk . . . Incidentally, I was able to repay one of the girls later in the Pechora camp: in '35 she got taken in following the death of Kirov, and she had just about reached the end of her tether doing hard labour, and I got her fixed up in the tailoring shop."

"Should we begin to mix the mortar?" Pavlo asked the gang-leader in a whisper.

The gang-leader didn't hear him.

"I reached home one night through the back garden, and I left the same night. I took my little brother with me, and we went off to a warmer spot, Frunze. I had nothing to feed him on – or myself. In a street in Frunze, they were boiling some asphalt in a cauldron, and there were a bunch of riff-raff sitting around. I went up to them: 'Listen, gentlemen of the streets! Take my little brother, and give him an education, teach him how to live!' They took him. I'm sorry I didn't go with them . . ."

"And you never saw your brother again?" asked the captain.

Tyurin yawned.

"No, never saw him again." He yawned once more. "Well, lads, don't vex yourselves! We'll make ourselves at home in the power-station. Those who are mixing the mortar had better get going, don't wait for the hooter."

That's how a gang runs. The authorities couldn't get a prisoner to work even in working-hours, but a gang-leader can tell them to work in the break, and they will. Because he fed them, the gang-leader. And he wasn't getting them to work simply for fun.

If they began to mix the mortar only when the hooter went, then what would the masons do?

Shukhov sighed and got up.

"I'll go and hack off the ice."

He took with him a small axe and a brush, and a mason's hammer for laying, a batten, some twine and a plumb.

Kilgas' ruddy face looked at Shukhov and grimaced as if to say why should he jump up before his gang-leader. Of course, Kilgas didn't have to think about ways of feeding the gang. It didn't concern him, the old bald head, if he got a couple of hundred grams of bread less – he could manage on his parcels.

Nevertheless, he got up. He understood: you couldn't hold back the gang on account of yourself.

"Hang on, Ivan, and I'll come with you!" he said.

That's it, fat-face, that's it. If you'd been working for yourself, you'd have been on your feet a damn sight quicker.

(And Shukhov was also in a hurry because he wanted to get hold of that plumb before Kilgas; it was the only one they'd got from the tool-shop.)

"Will three be enough to lay blocks?" Pavlo asked the gang-leader. "Should we put somebody else on the job? Or won't there be enough mortar?"

The gang-leader frowned and thought a while.

"I'll be the fourth man myself, Pavlo. And you stay here with the mortar. It's a big box, we'll put six men on the job. And take the mortar out of one end when it is ready, and mix up the new stuff at the other end. Not a moment's interruption!"

Pavlo jumped up. He was a young man, his blood was fresh, camp life had not reduced him too far yet, his face was still plump from eating Ukrainian dumplings at home.

"If you lay the blocks," he said, "then I'll mix the mortar for you myself – and we'll see who's faster Where's the longest shovel around here?"

That's how a gang runs. Pavlo used to shoot in the forest, and had made night-raids on villages – why should he knock himself out with work in the camp? But for the gang-leader – that was another thing.

Shukhov went up with Kilgas, and they heard Senka creaking up the ladder behind them. Deaf as he was, he had guessed what was going on.

The previous lot had only made a start on laying the blocks on the walls of the second storey: three rows all round, a little higher here and there. This was when laying was fastest – from the knee to the chest, without the use of steps.

The steps which had been there earlier, and the planks – they had all been taken by other prisoners. Some had been carried off to other buildings, some had been burnt – just so that no other gang would have them. Tomorrow they would have to nail some planks together, or they'd be unable to get on with the job.

One could see a long way from the top of the power-station: the whole site snow-covered all round and deserted (the prisoners were hidden away, trying to get warm before the hooter went), the black watch-towers, the sharpened poles for the barbed wire. One could not see the wire itself by looking at it against the sun –

only away from it. The sun shone very brightly, and it hurt one's eyes.

And not far off was the power engine, blackening the sky with its smoke – and breathing heavily. It always made that great wheezing noise before sounding the hooter. There it went. They hadn't got down to work so early, after all.

"Hey, Stakhanovite! Hurry up with that plumb!" Kilgas shouted.

"See how much ice there's on your wall! You going to chip it off before evening?" Shukhov retorted sarcastically. "Your trowel won't be much use to you until you do!"

They planned to start on those walls which they had allocated to each other before dinner, but now the gang-leader shouted up from below:

"Hey, lads! We'll work in pairs so that the mortar doesn't freeze in the hods. Shukhov, you take Klevshin on your wall, and I'll work with Kilgas. But for the moment Gopchik can take my place and clean up Kilgas' wall."

Shukhov and Kilgas exchanged looks. It was true. It would be quicker.

They seized their axes.

And no longer did Shukhov see that distant view where the sun shone on the snow – or did he see his fellow-prisoners wandering over the site from the places where they'd been keeping warm – some to dig holes which they hadn't finished in the morning, some to reinforce mesh, some to put up beams in the work-shops. Shukhov saw only his wall – from the corner on his left where the blocks rose in steps, higher than his waist, to the right-hand corner where his wall joined up with Kilgas'. He showed Senka where to take off the ice, and himself hacked away at it eagerly with the head and blade of his axe so that chips of ice flew all around him and into his face even. He worked well and swiftly, but his thoughts were not on his immediate work. His thoughts and his eyes were concentrated on the wall below the ice, the outside wall of the power-station, two blocks thick. He didn't know the mason who had worked on that part of the wall before him, but he was either an idiot or an incompetent. Shukhov felt at one with the wall as if it were his own. There – there was a gap which it would be impossible to level out in one row; he'd have to do it in three, each time adding the mortar a little more thickly. And here the outer wall was swelling out – it would take two rows to straighten that. He divided up the wall in his mind into the place where he'd lay blocks, from the left-hand corner, the stretch Senka was working on – on the right, and as far as where Kilgas was. There, on the corner on the right, he reckoned that Kilgas wouldn't hold back, would lay a few blocks for Senka to make things easier for him. And before they finished tinkering in the corner, Shukhov on his side would have more than half the wall up so that his pair did not fall behind. He made a note as to how many blocks he would have to lay where. And as soon as they began to get the blocks up, he shouted at Alyoshka:

"Bring 'em to me! Put 'em down here – and here!"

Senka finished hacking off the ice, and Shukhov got hold of a wire brush, gripped it in both hands, and started along the wall, scrubbing to and fro, cleaning the top row of blocks, especially the joints, until they were a light greyish colour like dirty snow.

The gang-leader climbed up and, while Shukhov was still busy cleaning with the wire-brush, set up his batten at the corner. Shukhov and Kilgas had set theirs up on the edges of the wall some time before.

"Hey!" Pavlo shouted from below. "Anybody still alive up there? We're coming up with the mortar!"

Shukhov began to sweat. He hadn't stretched his twine over the blocks yet! He got moving fast, and decided to stretch the twine not over one row, not over two rows, but over three at once, leaving some room to spare. And in order to make things easier for Senka, he took a bit of the outer wall from him, and left him a bit of the inside wall.

Stretching the twine along the top, he explained to Senka by words and signs where he was to lay. He understood, deaf as he was. Biting his lips, he squinted in the direction of the gang-leader's wall as if to say: "We'll give it to 'em! We'll keep up!" He laughed.

They were bringing the mortar up the ladder. Four pairs of men would be bringing it up. The gang-leader decided that the mortar should not be emptied from the hods beside the masons – it would only freeze before they had had time to lay it. The carriers were to put the hods down straight away – and the two masons on each part of the wall would take out the mortar and lay it immediately. Meanwhile, the carriers, in order that they shouldn't freeze up there doing nothing, would carry the blocks to the layers. As soon as the hods were empty, then without any break in time the first pair would go down, and another pair would come up. Then, at the bottom, any mortar which had frozen in the empty hods would be thawed out by the stove – and the men would thaw themselves out, too.

They brought up the hods two at a time – one for Kilgas' wall and one for Shukhov's. The mortar steamed in the cold, although it wasn't really warm at all. You had to get a move on, slapping it on the wall with a trowel – or else it would harden up. If it did, then you had to hit it with the side of a hammer, you wouldn't get it off with a trowel. And if you laid your block a little off centre, then it'd freeze instantly and set out of place – and you'd have to knock it away with the head of your axe and chip off the mortar.

But Shukhov made no mistake. The blocks were not always the same. If one had a corner chipped or a broken edge or something else wrong with it, Shukhov would spot it immediately, and would see which way up to lay the block and the precise place on the wall to put it.

Shukhov scooped up some steaming mortar with his trowel, threw it into place, remembering where the joint was in the row below (it should be in the middle of the block he was going to lay on top). He threw on exactly enough mortar for one block, picked a block out of the pile (carefully, so as not to tear his mittens – easy to do that with blocks), levelled the mortar once more with his trowel – and then on with the block! He evened it out immediately, tapping it with the side of the trowel if it wasn't lying quite true – so that the outside wall would run plumb straight and the blocks lie level both lengthways and across. And the mortar would soon have frozen.

Now, if any of the mortar squeezed out from under the block, you had to scrape it off with the edge of your trowel as quickly as possible and chuck it over the wall (in summer it could be used to go under the next block, but now it was unthinkable). Then you took another look at the joint below – sometimes the block would not be whole, would have crumbled, and you would have to slap in some more mortar to fill up the gap; and you couldn't always simply lay the block down flat, but would have to slide it from side to side, and it was then you'd get the extra mortar coming out from between the block and its neighbour. One eye on the plumb. One eye on the laying surface. Down with the block. Next!

The work went well. Once he'd laid a couple of rows and ironed out the existing faults, then it'd be smooth going. But just now, he had to be as sharp-sighted as hell!

He slaved away on the outside row to meet Senka. Senka had parted company with the gang-leader at the corner, and was now working towards Shukhov.

Shukhov winked at the carriers – come on, come on, look lively! He was working at such a pace he didn't have time to wipe his nose.

When he and Senka came together, they began to

scoop mortar out of the same hod – and they soon exhausted it.

"Mortar!" Shukhov shouted over the wall.

"Coming!" Pavlo shouted back.

They brought up another hod, which was soon emptied – the unfrozen mortar, that is, for a lot had frozen to the sides of the hod. Get it out yourselves! There was no point in letting the frozen mortar accumulate in the box, since the carriers would have to be carrying it up and down all the time. Go on, get rid of it! Next!

Now Shukhov and the other masons had ceased to feel the cold. As a result of the speed and absorption with which they worked, the first wave of warmth had overtaken them – and they felt wet under their coats and jackets and shirts and undershirts. But not for a moment did they stop work, and gave themselves more and more to the task of laying. And after an hour they experienced that second wave of warmth – when the sweat dries on them. And their feet didn't feel cold, that was the main thing, and nothing else mattered. The light, piercing wind did not distract their thoughts from the job. Only Klevshin stamped his feet: he took size 46, poor fellow, and his felt boots weren't of the same size, and were tight on him anyway.

From time to time, the gang-leader would shout: "Mortar!", and Shukhov would shout the same thing. If a fellow is working really hard, he becomes a kind of gang-leader over those working with him. It was up to Shukhov to keep up with the other pair, and he would have chased his own brother up the ladder with hods of mortar.

At first, since dinner, Buinovsky had carried mortar with Fetyukov. But the ladder was steep and slippery, and he hadn't done very well to begin with. Shukhov urged him on gently:

"A little quicker, captain! More blocks over here, captain!"

But while the captain became more expeditious with

each load, Fetyukov became more idle: the bastard would tilt the hods as he came up, allowing some of the mortar to spill out so that they would be lighter to carry.

Once Shukhov poked him in the back:

"Come on, you bloody swine! I'll bet you worked your men hard enough when you were a director in that office of yours!"

"Gang-leader!" the captain shouted. "Give me a man to work with! I can't carry anything with this piece of shit!"

The gang-leader transferred Fetyukov to hauling up blocks from the ground to the scaffolding – in a position where it would be possible to count how many blocks he handled; and put Alyoshka to work with the captain. Alyoshka was a quiet one, and would do whatever he was told, whoever told him.

"All hands on deck, then!" the captain shouted at him. "See how they're laying the blocks!"

Alyoshka smiled meekly:

"If we must work faster, then let's work faster. Anything you say."

And down the ladder they went.

A meek fellow like that was a treasure in any gang.

The gang-leader shouted to somebody below. It seemed that another load of blocks had arrived. Not one had turned up here for half a year, and now they were pouring in. This was the time to work – while they were bringing the blocks. It was the first day. It wouldn't be easy to cope later if they got held up.

The gang-leader was swearing at somebody else below. Something about the hoist. Shukhov wanted to know what was going on, but he had no time: he was levelling his wall. A couple of the carriers came up and told him that a fitter had arrived to repair the motor of the hoist, and with him, the superintendent of electrical works, himself not a prisoner. The fitter rummaged around inside the motor, the superintendent just looked on.

That was how it went: one man worked, the other just watched.

If they were able to repair the hoist now, they could use it to lift both the blocks and the mortar.

Shukhov was already laying his third row of blocks (and Kilgas had started his third as well) when up the ladder came another patrolling official – building foreman Der. A Muscovite. It was said he had worked in a ministry there.

Shukhov was standing close to Kilgas and he drew his attention to Der.

"Ugh!" Kilgas brushed the sight aside. "In general I have nothing to do with the officials, but if he slips on the ladder, then give me a call."

Now Der would stand behind the masons and watch them work. Shukhov just couldn't stand these prowlers. Trying to become an engineer, the pig's snout! Once he had tried to show Shukhov how to lay blocks – that had been a joke! You just build a house with your own two hands first, and then you can think of becoming an engineer – that was how Shukhov felt.

At Temgenovo there were no stone houses, all the huts were made of wood. The school-house was of wood, too – six-foot logs carried in from the forest. But in the camp they needed masons – so, Shukhov became a mason. A man who could use his hands in two trades would have no trouble acquiring another ten!

No, Der hadn't slipped on the ladder, although he had stumbled once. He almost ran up.

"Tyurin!" he shouted, his eyes popping out of his head. "Tyurin!"

Pavlo ran up the ladder behind him with the shovel he'd been using in his hands.

Der was wearing an ordinary camp coat, although it was new and clean. His cap was smart and made of leather, but it had a number on it, like everybody else's: B–731 in this case.

"Well?" The gang-leader approached him with his trowel in his hand, his cap tilted over one eye.

Something was up. Shukhov didn't want to miss anything, but the mortar was freezing in the hod. Shukhov went on laying, keeping his ears open.

"Well, what's this?" Der shouted, spitting saliva. "This isn't just a spell in the cells! This is a criminal matter, Tyurin! You'll get a third sentence for this!"

Only then did Shukhov twig what it was all about. He glanced at Kilgas – who had also realised. The roofing-felt! Der had seen the roofing felt on the windows.

Shukhov feared nothing for himself. His gang-leader would never betray him. But he did fear for Tyurin. For the gang he was like a father, for them – he was merely a pawn. For just such a thing as this they were quick to give a gang-leader a second term up here in the North.

Heavens, how the gang-leader's face twitched! How he threw down his trowel – and took a step towards Der! Der looked round – and Pavlo raised his shovel.

The shovel! He hadn't brought it up with him for nothing ...

And Senka, deaf though he was, understood: he moved forward, his hands on his hips. And he was a big fellow, that one.

Der blinked, looked worried and cast his eyes round for an escape route.

The gang-leader leaned towards Der and said quite quietly, although clearly enough to be heard up there:

"Your time for handing out sentences has passed, you rat! If you say a word, you bloodsucker, this'll be your last day. Get it!"

The gang-leader was shaking all over, and was unable to control himself.

And sharp-faced Pavlo looked Der straight in the eye – as sharp as a razor.

"Steady now, lads, take it easy!" Der turned pale — and moved further away from the ladder.

The gang-leader said not another word, straightened his cap, picked up his trowel and went back to his wall.

And Pavlo, with his shovel, walked slowly down the ladder.

Ever so slowly . . .

Der was frightened to remain up there, and frightened to go down. He went and stood by Kilgas.

Kilgas went on laying — carefully, like they weigh medicine in a chemist's shop; like a doctor and never in a hurry. He had his back to Der as if he didn't know he was there.

Der crept up to the gang-leader. Where was all his pride now?

"What shall I say to the superintendent, Tyurin?"

The gang-leader went on laying, and said without turning his head:

"Tell him that's how it was when we got here. We arrived — and that's how it was."

Der stood around a little longer. He realised that they were not going to kill him now. He walked around a bit, quietly, and put his hands in his pockets.

"Hey, S–854," he grumbled. "Why are you laying that mortar on so thin?"

He had to take it out on somebody. He couldn't find any fault with Shukhov's joints or straightness — so it was the mortar that was too thin.

"Allow me to point out," Shukhov lisped, smirking, "that if I laid the mortar on any thicker now, this whole power-station would leak like hell in the spring."

"You're a mason, so listen to what a foreman has to tell you," Der said with a frown, and blew out his cheeks, which was a habit of his.

Well, maybe it was a little thin here and there, and he could have used a bit more — but only if he had been laying in ordinary conditions and not in winter But people should have some understanding. Output was important. But what was the point of explaining it to an ignoramus like Der, anyway!

And Der went slowly down the ladder.

"You get that hoist put right for me!" the gang-leader shouted after him from the wall. "What do you think we are – donkeys? Hauling blocks up to the second storey by hand!"

"You'll get paid for carrying them up," Der said from the ladder, but mildly.

"Yes, but paid for carrying them in wheelbarrows. Could you push a wheelbarrow up that ladder? We should get paid for carrying them up by hand."

"You don't think I'd mind, do you? But the book-keepers would never pass it."

"Bookkeepers! I've got a whole gang working to keep four masons at it. How much do you think we're going to earn?" the gang-leader shouted, without interrupting his laying.

"Mortar!" he shouted down.

"Mortar!" Shukhov echoed him. They'd finished levelling the third row and could get going on the fourth. He should stretch the twine along the row again, but he reckoned he'd manage without it this time.

Der went off across the site, looking somewhat shrunken. He'd warm up in the office. He couldn't have been feeling too good. He should think twice before mixing with a wolf like Tyurin. He should try to keep on good terms with gang-leaders like him, and then he'd have nothing to worry about. He wasn't asked to do any really serious work, he got the highest category of rations, he lived in a separate cabin. What else did he want? Giving himself airs like that, and trying to be clever.

A pair of carriers came up from below to say that the superintendent of electrical works had gone, the fitter had gone – and it was impossible to mend the hoist.

So on with the donkey work.

In all the many jobs Shukhov had done in camp life,

the machinery had either broken down itself or had been smashed by the prisoners. They had once broken a log-conveyer by shoving a pole under the chain and pressing down on it. In order to get a breather. They'd been piling up log after log without a break.

"More blocks! More blocks!" shouted the gang-leader, flying into a temper. "And go fuck your mothers, all of you!"

"Pavlo's asking how you're off for mortar?" they shouted up from below.

"Mix some more!"

"We've got half a box mixed!"

"Well, mix another!"

They were really moving now! They were going along the fifth row. They'd had to bend themselves double on the first row, and now the wall was up to their chests. It wasn't so hard to get on, with no windows or doors, just two blank walls joined to each other and a lot of blocks. They should have stretched the twine in the higher position, but it was too late.

"Gang 82 have gone to hand in their tools," Gopchik announced.

The gang-leader's eyes flashed at him.

"Get on with your work, you little mushroom! Keep those blocks moving!"

Shukhov looked about. Yes, the sun was setting. It was all red and seemed to be sinking into a greyish haze. And they were really getting a move on – couldn't have gone faster. They'd begun on the fifth row now – and they should have time to finish it, and level it off.

The carriers looked like winded horses. The captain had turned quite grey. He was, after all, round about forty.

It was getting colder. Even though his hands were working all the time, Shukhov's fingers were beginning to feel numb through his ragged mittens. And the cold was getting into his left boot. He stamped his foot up and down.

No longer did he have to bend down to reach the wall now, but he had to break his back each time he reached for a block or a scoop of mortar.

"Hey, you lads!" Shukhov badgered them. "Get me some blocks onto the wall here! Put 'em up on the wall!"

The captain would have been glad to help, but he lacked the strength. He wasn't used to the work. But Alyoshka said:

"All right, Ivan Denisovitch. Show me where to put 'em."

Alyoshka would never refuse, would do everything asked of him. If everybody in the world had been like him, Shukhov would be as well. If a man asks for something, then why refuse him? Those Baptists were right.

All over the site, and as far as the power-station, could be clearly heard the sound of the rail being banged. Knocking-off time! They still had some mortar left. Ah, when you tried hard . . .

"Give me some mortar! Give me some mortar!" the gang-leader shouted.

And a new box of mortar had only just been mixed! Now they'd have to go on laying, there was nothing else for it: if they didn't empty the box, then tomorrow they'd have to smash the whole box to pieces, the mortar would have set so hard, and they'd never be able to hack it out with picks.

"Come on, brothers, don't fail me!" Shukhov shouted.

Kilgas hated this. He did not like rush jobs. But he pressed on. What else could he do?

Pavlo ran up the ladder with a hod, and with a trowel in one hand. To help with the laying. There were five trowels at work now.

Now they'd have to watch out where the blocks met! Shukhov always picked out with his eye beforehand the size of block he was going to want. He pushed a hammer into Alyoshka's hand and said:

"Go on, knock this one to size for me!"

You can't work well if you're in too much of a hurry. Now that everybody else was speeding away, Shukhov slowed down a bit and observed the wall carefully. He pushed Senka over to the left-hand side, and himself went to the main corner on the right. If the wall didn't join up properly or if the corner went wrong – that would be half a day's work putting it right tomorrow.

"Stop!" He pushed Pavlo away from a block and righted it himself. And from there, in the corner, he saw that Senka's bit was beginning to sag. He rushed over to Senka and straightened it out with a couple of blocks.

The captain, like an old carthorse, hauled up more mortar.

"Two more hods!" he shouted.

The captain was tottering on his legs, but he carried on. Shukhov was reminded of a horse he had once had. Shukhov had cared for it well, but it had worked itself to death. Then they'd skinned the hide off it.

The upper edge of the sun was going down below the horizon now. They didn't need Gopchik to tell them that not only had all the gangs handed in their tools, but also that they were moving in a wave towards the guard-room. (Nobody went there immediately after the signal went – they'd have been fools to stand around freezing. They all sat back in their shelters. Then came the moment, agreed among the gang-leaders, when all the gangs should pour out together. If there hadn't been this agreement, the prisoners were so stubborn, they would have sat around in their shelters until midnight, waiting for another gang to make the first move.)

Tyurin came to his senses and realised that he had left things very late. The man in the tool-shop would be cursing him like mad, for sure.

"Hey!" he shouted. "Don't worry about that shit! Carriers! Let down the ladder, and scrape out the box into that hole there, and cover it up with snow so that nobody will see! And you, Pavlo, take a couple of men, collect the tools and go and hand them in! I'll send the remaining three trowels with Gopchik, and we'll finish these last two hods."

Everyone got going. They took Shukhov's hammer and unfastened his twine. The carriers and the block-shifters hastened down the ladder to the machine-room where they'd been making the mortar – there was nothing more for them to do up there. Three masons remained on top – Kilgas, Klevshin and Shukhov. The gang-leader wanted to see how much they had achieved. He was content.

"Not bad for half a day's work, eh? And without a fucking hoist at that?"

Shukhov noticed that Kilgas still had a little mortar left. He was reluctant to waste it – but was worried that the gang-leader would get blasted by the man in the tool-shop for handing back the trowels so late.

"Listen, lads," he said, "give your trowels to Gop-chik. Mine is not accounted for, so I don't have to give it back, and I'll finish up the job with it."

The gang-leader laughed:

"How can we ever let you go free? The camp will be in a sorry state without you!"

Shukhov laughed as well, and went on laying.

Kilgas took the trowels. Senka started handing blocks to Shukhov, and they poured Kilgas' mortar into Shukhov's hod.

Gopchik ran across the site to the tool-shop, trying to catch up with Pavlo. And the rest of Gang 104 started out across the site without the gang-leader. A gang-leader is a force to be reckoned with, but the guards were a force stronger by far. They recorded those who were late and that meant the cells.

There was a terrible crowd around the guard-room. Everybody had gathered there. It looked as if the escort guards had come out and had started to count.

(The prisoners were counted twice on the way out:

once when the gates were still shut, in order that the guards should be able to open them; and again when the gates were open and the prisoners were passing through them. And if the guards thought that they had made a mistake, then they counted again outside the gates.)

"To hell with the mortar!" the gang-leader said, waving his arm. "Chuck it over the wall!"

"You'd better go, gang-leader! Go, you'll be needed over there!" (Shukhov usually called the gang-leader Andrei Prokofyevitch, but now, after his work, he felt on a kind of par with the gang-leader. Not so that he thought to himself: "Well, I'm your equal!" but he simply knew that it was so.) And as the gang-leader descended the ladder with resolute tread, Shukhov called after him: "Why do the swine give us such a short working day? You've only got going on your work, and they knock you off!"

Shukhov was left with deaf Senka now. You didn't talk much with him, but you didn't need to: he was smarter than them all, he understood without words.

Slap on the mortar! Down with the block! Press down! Check! Mortar. Block. Mortar. Block . . .

The boss had said not to worry about the mortar – chuck it over the wall and push off. But Shukhov wasn't made that way, and eight years of camp life hadn't altered him: he still worried about every little thing and every piece of work – and he hated waste.

Mortar. Block. Mortar. Block . . .

"We've finished, fuck it!" Senka shouted. "Let's be off!"

He seized a hod and went down the ladder.

But Shukhov – and the guards could have put the dogs on him now, it would have made no difference – ran back to have a look round. Not bad. He ran over and looked along the wall – to the left, to the right. His eye was true. Good and straight! His hands were still good. He ran down the ladder.

Senka was already out of the machine-room and running down the rise on which the power-station was situated.

"Come on, come on!" he shouted over his shoulder.

"Run on, I'm coming!" Shukhov waved back at him.

And he went into the machine-room. He couldn't simply throw down his trowel like that. Perhaps, tomorrow, Shukhov would not be sent to this place, but the gang would be ordered to the Socialist Community Centre, perhaps he wouldn't come back here for six months or so – and would that be that with the trowel? No, he'd do his best to hang on to it.

Both the stoves in the room had been extinguished. It was dark. Frightening. Not frightening because of the dark, but because everybody had left, because he might be the only one not to be counted at the guard-room, and the escort guards would beat him.

He looked all around, spotted a large stone in a corner, rolled it back, slipped his trowel in and covered it up. That was that!

Now to catch up with Senka. But Senka had only gone a hundred yards or so and was waiting for him. Klevshin would never leave you in the lurch. If you had to answer for anything, you'd answer together.

They ran off side by side – the short and the tall. Senka was half a head taller than Shukhov, and it was a big enough head at that.

There are some people with nothing better to do than chase each other round a stadium of their own free will. Let them try it, the devils, after a full day's work, with their backs still not straightened out, their mittens wet, in worn out felt boots – and in the freezing cold.

They were panting like rabid dogs, and all that could be heard was the sound of their heavy breathing.

Well, the gang-leader was at the guard-room, and he'd explain for them.

Now they were running straight towards the crowd, and it was frightening.

Hundreds of voices yelling at them at once: "Fuckers! Bastards! Cunts! Fuckers!" Five hundred men raging at you – it certainly was a frightening thing.

But the main thing was what the escort guards would do.

No, they weren't going to do anything. The gang-leader was there, in the last row. It meant that he had explained, had taken the blame on himself.

But the lads swore and yelled obscenities – and made such a row that even Senka heard a lot of it; and he took a deep breath and roared back with all his might! All his life he had been a quiet sort of person – but, now, how he bellowed! He shook his fists, and seemed ready to fight any and all comers. The men quietened down, and some of them laughed.

"Hey, Gang 104! We thought you had a deaf one among you?" somebody cried out. "We were just making sure."

Everybody laughed. Even the guards.

"Line up in fives!"

They didn't open the gates. They weren't sure enough of themselves. They pushed the crowd back from the gates. (Everybody surged up to the gates – as if, the idiots, they'd get out any quicker like that.)

"Line up in fives! One! Two! Three!"

And as each five was called, they moved forward a few yards.

While Shukhov was getting his breath back, he looked up – the moon had already risen and was scowling reddishly in the sky. Perhaps it was beginning to wane. Yesterday it had been much higher in the sky at this time.

Shukhov felt cheerful that everything had gone off so smoothly, and he poked the captain in the side and said:

"Listen, captain, where according to that science of yours does the old moon go to when it's through?"

"Where does it go? What do you mean? It simply isn't visible any more!"

Shukhov shook his head and laughed:

"Well, if it's not visible, how do you know it's there?"

"So, according to you," said the captain, astonished, "we get a new moon every month?"

"What's so strange about that? People are born every day, why shouldn't there be a new moon every four weeks?"

"Pfui!" the captain spat. "I've never met such a dumb sailor as you. So where do you think the old moon goes?"

"That's what I'm asking you – where?" Shukhov grinned.

"Well, where does it go, tell me?"

Shukhov sighed and said, hardly lisping:

"At home they used to say that God broke up the old moon for stars."

"What savages!" The captain laughed. "I've never heard such a thing! Do you believe in God, Shukhov?"

"Why not?" Shukhov replied, surprised. "When you hear Him thunder, you can't help believing in Him."

"And why do you think God does that, then?"

"Does what?"

"Break the moon up into stars?"

"Well, don't you understand?" Shukhov shrugged his shoulders. "The stars fall down from time to time, and it is necessary to fill the gaps."

"Turn round, you swine . . ." an escort guard shouted. "Get into line!"

The counting had got as far as them. The twelfth row of five of the fifty hundred moved forward, leaving only Buinovsky and Shukhov behind.

The escort guards were worried and began a discussion over the counting boards. Somebody missing? It had happened before! If only they would learn to count!

They had counted off 462, but they reckoned that it should have been 463.

They pushed everybody back from the gates again (they had pressed forward again) – and:

"Line up in fives! One! Two!"

The worst thing about these recounts was that they came out of the prisoners' time, not time which otherwise would have been spent working. They still had to go back across the steppe to the camp and then line up to be searched. Everybody from all the sites would race to get back to the camp as quickly as possible so as to be early in turn to be searched, and consequently quicker to get into camp. The first column to arrive back in camp had everything their own way: the mess-hall was at their disposal, they were the first to get their parcels, first to the "individual" kitchen, first to the store-room, first to the CES to collect letters or to the censor to hand in letters, to the infirmary, the barber's, the bath-house – they were first everywhere.

And the escort guards weren't sorry to see the back of them either – and hand them over to the camp. It wasn't much fun being a soldier either: a lot to do, not much time.

And now the count had gone wrong.

As the last rows of five began to move forward, it seemed to Shukhov that there would be three men left at the end. But no, there were two again.

The counters went to the Chief Escort Guard with their boards. There was a discussion. The Chief Escort Guard shouted:

"Gang-leader 104!"

Tyurin stepped forward half a pace:

"Here."

"Did you leave anybody at the power-station? Think."

"No."

"Think hard, or I'll knock your head off!"

"No, I'm sure."

But he glanced at Pavlo – could anybody have dropped off to sleep in the machine-room?

"Line up in gangs!" the Chief Escort Guard shouted.

They had formed into fives according to where they had been standing at the time, anybody with anybody. Now they began to move about and to re-form. Someone shouted: "Gang 76 – over here!" "Gang 13, this way!" somebody else shouted. And: "Gang 32 here!"

Gang 104 had been behind everybody else, and they grouped together there. Shukhov noticed that nobody in the gang had anything in his hands. They had been so busy working, the fools, that they had not collected any firewood. Then he saw that two of them – only two – were carrying small bundles.

They played this game every day: before knocking-off time the prisoners would collect chips, sticks and broken laths, and tie them together with bits of rag or old string to take back to camp. The first raid on these bundles took place at the guard-room – by a superintendent or one of the foremen. If one of these was standing there, he would order the bundles to be thrown down (millions of roubles had already gone up in smoke, and they thought they could make up for the waste with chips of wood). But the prisoners' calculation was that if every man from every gang brought back with him even a stick or two, then the barracks would be somewhat warmer. The orderlies were given five kilograms of coal dust per stove, and you couldn't get much warmth out of that. So the men would break up the pieces of wood, or saw them short, and stuff them under their coats. In this way they would elude the superintendent.

The escort guards on the site never ordered the men to drop their bundles until they'd got them back to camp. They also needed firewood, but it was impossible for them to carry it. For one thing, they were wearing uniform, and for another their hands were occupied – with tommy-guns with which to shoot at the prisoners.

103

But when they got back to camp, the order went out: "Row Such-and-Such to Row Such-and-Such, drop your bundles here!" But they robbed mercifully: they had to leave something for the camp warders, and for the prisoners themselves, who would not otherwise bring any wood back.

So every prisoner brought something back with him every day. You never knew when you might get it through or when it might be taken from you.

While Shukov was looking around to see if there were any odd bits of wood to pick up, the gang-leader finished counting the gang and reported to the Chief Escort Guard:

"Gang 104 all present!"

Tsesar had left his fellow office-workers to join the gang. His pipe glowing red as he puffed away at it, and his black moustache tinged with frost, he asked:

"Well, captain, and how are things?"

A man who's warm cannot understand one who's freezing – or he wouldn't ask silly questions like that – "How are things?" indeed.

"Well," the captain said, shrugging his shoulders. "I've worked so hard I can hardly straighten my back."

And you might give me something to smoke was the implication.

Tsesar did give him something to smoke. The captain was the only man in the gang he kept close to, and to him more than anyone else was he able to unburden his soul.

"One man missing in Gang 32! Gang 32!" everybody began to shout.

The second-in-command of Gang 32 dashed off with a young fellow with him to search the repair-shops. And in the crowd people kept asking: "Who is it? What's happening?" The news reached Shukhov that it was the short, dark Moldavian. But which short, dark Moldavian? Not the Moldavian who, it was said, had been a Rumanian spy, a real spy?

104

Spies – there were up to five spies in every gang, but they were not necessarily the real thing. Their records showed them as spies, but they had probably been simply prisoners-of-war. Shukhov was that kind of spy.

But the Moldavian – he had been the real thing.

The Chief Escort Guard looked down at his list, and his face blackened. If a real spy had indeed got away – then the Chief Escort Guard would be for it.

In the crowd, everybody, including Shukhov, went mad. Who did he think he was, this vulture, this swine, bastard, shit, fucker? The sky was already dark, and what light there was came from the moon. The stars were out, and the night frost was gathering strength – and now this Moldavian bastard was missing! Hadn't the shit worked enough that day? Weren't the regulation hours – eleven hours from dawn to dusk – sufficiently long for him? Well, maybe the public prosecutor would add to them!

It was extraordinary to Shukhov that anyone could work so hard as not to notice the signal to knock off.

Shukhov had completely forgotten that he himself had been working like that only recently – that he had been irritated that everybody else had collected around the guard-room excessively early. Now he was frozen stiff like the rest of them, furious like the rest of them, and it seemed to him that if that Moldavian kept them hanging around for another half hour, and if the escort guards gave him to the crowd – then they'd tear him to pieces, like wolves would a lamb!

The cold was really biting into them now! Nobody stood still – either they stamped their feet up and down where they stood, or walked two or three paces backwards and forwards.

People were discussing whether the Moldavian could have escaped. Well, if he had got away during the day, that was one thing, but if he had hidden and was waiting for the escort guards to leave their watch-towers, he'd have a long time to wait. If there were no traces

105

under the wire to indicate his point of escape — they'd scour the site for three days, and leave the escort guards in the watch-towers for three days, until they found him. Or a week, if necessary. That was as it was laid down, as all the old prisoners knew. In general, if somebody got away, the guards' lives were made hell, and they were kept at it without sleep or food. Sometimes, they got so mad that the escaper wouldn't be brought back alive.

Tsesar was arguing with the captain:

"For example, do you remember the shot when the pince-nez were hanging from the ship's rigging?"

"Mm . . ." the captain said, smoking.

"Or the perambulator going down the steps — bumping, bumping . . ."

"Yes . . . but life on board is rendered somewhat artificially."

"Yes, you see, but we have been spoiled by modern camera techniques . . ."

"And the maggots in the meat crawled around just like rainworms. Surely they weren't as large as that?"

"But in cinema you can't show things like that much smaller!"

"Well, I think if they brought that meat to the camp instead of the fish we get, and shoved it straight into the cauldron even without cleaning it or washing it, then I reckon we'd be . . ."

"Aaaa . . .!" the prisoners yelled. "Oooo . . .!"

They saw three figures darting out of the repair-shops — which meant that one of them was the Moldavian.

The crowd at the gates booed.

And as the three hastened nearer, they yelled:

"Rat! Shit! No-good bastard! Cunt! Swine! Vulture!"

And Shukhov also shouted:

"Rat!"

It was no joke to rob five hundred men of more than half an hour.

His head down, the Moldavian ran like a little mouse.

"Halt!" an escort guard shouted, and began to write. "K–460, where have you been?"

The guard walked over to him and turned the butt of his rifle towards him.

Everybody in the crowd was shouting:

"Bastard! Puke! Swine!"

Others, seeing that the guard was on the point of swinging the butt of his rifle, fell silent.

The Moldavian said nothing, hung his head and backed away from the guard. The second-in-command of Gang 32 stepped forward:

"The bastard climbed up the scaffolding to do some plastering. But he hid from me, found a warm spot up there and went to sleep."

And he hit him with his fist in the neck and in the face! But, with these blows, he pushed the Moldavian further away from the guard.

The Moldavian staggered back, and then a Hungarian from Gang 32 leaped out and kicked him in the back again and again!

This was rougher than spying. Any fool can be a spy. A spy has a clean and happy life. But try spending ten years in a punishment camp!

The guard lowered his rifle.

The Chief Escort Guard yelled:

"Get back from the gates! Line up in fives!"

So the dogs were going to have another count! What was the point, when the situation had now been made clear? The prisoners began to groan. All the anger they felt for the Moldavian was now directed towards the guards. They began to boo and wouldn't move away from the gates. "What's this?" the Chief Escort Guard bawled. "So you want to sit in the snow? That's all right by me, and I'll keep you there until morning!"

And he would, too. He'd had them on the snow many times before. They'd even had to lie down – "On your faces! Release safety-catches!" The prisoners knew all about it. They began slowly to move away from the gates.

"Back! Back!" an escort guard shouted.

"Why the hell do you push up against the gates, anyway, you idiots?" people at the back shouted at those in front. And they moved back under the pressure.

"Line up in fives! One! Two! Three!"

The moon was fully up by now. It was shining brightly, and the reddish colour it had had before had gone. It was a quarter the way up the sky. Their evening had gone! That damned Moldavian! The damned guards! This damned life!

When the men in front had been counted, they turned and stood on tiptoe to see if there were two or three people left in the last five. On this they felt their lives now depended.

It seemed to Shukhov that there were going to be four people left in the last five. He was sick with fear, If there was one extra person, then they'd have another recount! But it turned out that Fetyukov, that jackal, had been bumming a smoke off the captain, had forgotten what he was supposed to be doing, and had been late to return to his five – which was why he was now at the back, looking like an extra man.

The Chief Escort Guard's assistant angrily gave Fetyukov a sock on the neck.

Excellent!

So in the last five there were three men. Thank God the count had come out all right!

"Back from the gates!" one of the escort guards shouted again.

And this time the prisoners did not grumble, for they could see the guards coming out of the guard-room to cordon off an area on the other side of the gates.

Which meant that they would be letting them through.

None of the foremen was about, nor a superintendent, so the prisoners were able to carry their firewood.

The gates were thrown open. There, on the other side, by some wooden railings, stood the Chief Escort Guard with a checker.

"One! Two! Three!"

If they achieved the same count, then the guards would come down from the watch-towers.

But what a distance it was for them to trudge back across the site from those towers! It was only when the last prisoner had been led off the site, and the numbers had been found to tally, that they telephoned the watch-towers to say it was all right to come down. A Chief Escort Guard with any intelligence would get the column on the move immediately, because he knew that the prisoners had nowhere to run to, and that the guards from the watch-towers could catch up the column easily enough. But there were some stupid enough to be frightened that there wouldn't be enough armed men to oppose the prisoners if necessary, and these waited until the guards had made the journey across the site from their watch-towers.

They had one such dolt of a Chief Escort Guard on today. He waited.

The prisoners had been out in the cold all day and were already half dead with it. And now, after they had knocked off, to have to hang around for another whole hour! It was not so much the cold that got them but the loss of their evening. They wouldn't be able to do any of the things they wanted to do in camp.

"And how do you come to know so much about life in the British Navy?" Shukhov heard someone in the adjacent five asking the captain.

"Well, you see, I spent nearly a whole month aboard an English cruiser. Had my own cabin. I was attached to a convoy as a liaison officer. And then, if you please, after the war some English admiral — the devil must have got into him — sent me a souvenir gift inscribed: 'As a token of gratitude'. I was staggered and cursed like crazy! So here I am — in the same boat as the rest of you ... It's a small pleasure being shut up alongside Bendera's lot."

It was strange. Strange to see the barren steppe, the deserted site, the snow shining in the moonlight. The guards had already taken up their positions – ten yards apart, guns at the ready. A black herd of prisoners, and among them, wearing the same sort of coat as everybody else, S–311 – a man to whom life without gold epaulettes had been unknown to him, who'd hobnobbed with an English admiral, and who was now carrying hods with Fetyukov.

How possible it is to change the circumstances of a man's life ...

The escort guards were ready now. But no "sermon" this time, just:

"Quick march! Hurry up, then!"

To hell with your "Hurry up, then!" Now! They were sure to be the last column to arrive at camp, so there was no point in hurrying. Every one of the prisoners understood this, and there was no need to talk about it: you've held us back – now we'll hold you back, and doubtless you're thinking about getting warm, too ...

"Move faster!" the Chief Escort Guard shouted. "faster, those in front!"

To hell with your "Move faster!" The prisoners walked on at a regular pace, heads lowered, as if on the way to a funeral. We've nothing to lose now: however fast we go, we'll still be the last back in camp. He hasn't treated us with any sort of consideration – so now he can yell his head off!

The Chief Escort Guard went on shouting: "Move faster!" but he realised that the prisoners wouldn't increase their pace. And there was no excuse to shoot at them: they were proceeding in fives, in column, peaceably. The Chief Escort Guard had no power to force the prisoners to go more quickly. (In the mornings it was that alone that saved them, and they proceeded to

110

work as slowly as they could. A man in a hurry wouldn't last his time out in the camp – he'd sweat himself into his grave.)

So on they went, regularly and deliberately. The snow crunched under their boots. Some talked quietly, others didn't talk at all. Shukhov tried to remember if there was anything he hadn't done in camp that morning which he should have done. And he remembered – the infirmary! Curious that he should have forgotten about the infirmary entirely while he was working.

The infirmary would be about open by now. If he missed his supper, he could still get there in time. But now he hardly felt any pain. And they probably wouldn't even bother to take his temperature. It would be a waste of time to go. He'd got through without the help of the doctors. Those doctors could land you in your grave in no time.

He gave up the idea of the infirmary now, and began to think how he could add to his supper. His hopes were concentrated on the fact that Tsesar might get a parcel – it was time he did.

Suddenly, the progress of the column of prisoners began to alter. The column began to sway, broke from its regular pace, lurched forward, and there was a buzz of excitement all along it – and now the fives at the back, where Shukhov was, were no longer treading on the heels of those in front of them, but were running to keep up. A few yards at walking pace, and then they had to run again.

As the back of the column passed over a rise, Shukhov could see, over to the right of them, far across the steppe, another dark column moving diagonally across their own course. They must have spotted Shukhov's column, for they also seemed to be stepping out.

The other column could only be from the machine factory, and there were about three hundred men in it. It meant that they had had tough luck, too, and had been kept back. Shukhov wondered why. It sometimes happened that they were held back to finish repairs on some machine or other. But it wasn't too bad for them, they worked inside in the warm all day.

Well, who would win? Shukhov's column began to run, quite openly, and even the escort guards broke into a fast trot. The Chief Escort Guard yelled:

"No straggling! Keep up there at the back! Keep up!"

What the hell are you shouting for? Can't you see we're keeping up?

And everybody forgot what he had been talking or thinking about. One idea dominated: to get back to camp before the other column.

"We must beat 'em! We must beat 'em!"

Everything was now confused. The sweet had become sour, the sour sweet. The guards were no longer the enemies of the prisoners, but the friends. The enemy – the enemy was the other column.

All at once they felt more cheerful, and their anger passed.

"Get on! Get on!" the men at the back shouted at those in front.

Their column had now reached one of the streets leading to the camp, and the column from the machine factory had passed out of sight behind a housing block. It was a blind race.

They were going down the middle of the street now, and the way was easier. And for the escort guards there was nothing to stumble over at the sides of the column. They were bound to beat the others!

There was another reason why they had to beat the column from the machine factory: the men from there got an especially thorough searching at the camp guardroom. Since the time people started to cut each other's throat in the camp, the authorities reckoned that knives were being made in the machine factory and smuggled into the camp from there. So the machine factory boys got a real going over at the entrance to the camp. In late autumn, when the ground was already beginning to freeze up, the searchers had shouted at them:

"Off with your boots, those from the machine factory! Hold your boots in your hands!"

And they'd get searched in their bare feet.

And even now, notwithstanding the frost, they would shout at random:

"You there, take off your right boot! And you – your left boot!"

And the prisoner would take off his boot, and have to hop around on one leg, and turn his boot upside down and shake out the foot-cloth to show that there was no knife hidden in it.

Shukhov had heard – he didn't know if it was true or not – that in the summer some lads from the machine factory had brought back to the camp a couple of volley-ball posts, both of which had been stuffed with knives! Now, from time to time, a knife did show up in the camp here and there.

So they were half running when they passed the new club-house, another housing block and the wood-factory – and reached the turning which led straight to the camp guard-room.

"Hooo ... ooo!" shouted the column in a single voice.

This was the place where the roads merged – and the column from the machine factory was 150 yards behind, on the right!

Now it was plain sailing. Everybody in the column was delighted. As delighted as a hare which finds it can still frighten the life out of a frog.

And there was the camp – just as they had left it in the morning: night now, like night then. Lights were shining over the continuous fence, and they were especially bright around the guard-room, and the searching area was as light as if the sun were out.

But they still hadn't got to the guard-room ...

"Halt!" the assistant to the Chief Escort Guard

113

shouted. And handing his tommy-gun to one of the guards, he ran up close to the column (the guards weren't allowed to go near the prisoners with their guns): "All those standing on the right with firewood in their hands – throw it down to their right!"

Those on the outside had been carrying firewood with no attempt to conceal it. One bundle flew through the air, another, a third. Some tried to hang on to their bundles by passing them to the inside of the column, but their neighbours went for them:

"Chuck it down, or they'll take it off everybody else! Go on, chuck it down!"

Who is the prisoner's worst enemy? Another prisoner. If only the prisoners didn't fight with each other, then . . .

"Quick march!" the assistant to the Chief Escort Guard shouted.

And they proceeded towards the guard-room.

Five roads converged on the guard-room. An hour earlier, all the other columns had gathered here. If the place where these five roads met had been made up, then it would have been here – by the guard-room and searching area – that the main square of a future town would be sited. And then demonstrations would have taken place here, just as now the columns poured in from sites in every direction from the camp.

The warders were warming themselves inside the guard-room. They came out and stood opposite the prisoners.

"Open your coats and jackets!"

And the prisoners raised their arms, ready to be felt and searched, and slapped down the sides. The same sort of thing as in the morning.

But it wasn't so bad undoing their coats and jackets now, for they were nearly home.

Yes, they all spoke that word – "home".

There was no time in a prisoner's day to recall any other home.

114

While the men at the head of the column were being searched, Shukhov went up to Tsesar and said:

"Tsesar Markovitch! As soon as I'm through, I'll run straight over to the parcels' office and keep a place in the queue for you."

Tsesar turned to Shukhov, the ends of his black moustache still tinged with frost:

"Why should you do that, Ivan Denisovitch? Maybe there won't be a parcel."

"Well, if there isn't, what harm will it do me? I'll wait there ten minutes, and if you don't show up, I'll go back to the barracks."

(Shukhov was reckoning that if, indeed, Tsesar did not come, somebody else might to whom he could sell his place in the queue.)

It was clear that Tsesar was longing for a parcel:

"Well, all right, Ivan Denisovitch, you run over and get a place. But don't wait longer than ten minutes."

It was approaching Shukhov's turn to be searched. Today he had nothing to hide from the searcher, and he would step up fearlessly. He undid his coat, unhurryingly, and loosened the rope belt around his jacket.

And although he couldn't remember having anything on himself today which he shouldn't have, eight years of camp life had given him the habit of caution. He shoved his hand into the knee pocket on his trousers just to confirm to himself that it was empty as he knew it was.

And there was the piece of hacksaw blade – the piece of hacksaw blade he had picked up on the site today – because he had a thrifty nature – and which he had not had the least intention of bringing into the camp.

No intention at all, but now he'd got this far with it, surely it would be a pity to throw it away! He could fashion from it a small knife for mending boots or making clothes!

If he had meant to bring it in, he would have thought

115

hard as to where to hide it. But now there were only
two rows between him and the searchers, and already
the first of these rows of five was separating and moving
forward to be searched.

He had to make a decision quicker than the wind:
should he take cover behind the row in front of him and,
unnoticed, throw the thing into the snow (where they'd
find it later, but they'd never know where it had come
from), or should he try to get it through?

If they caught him with that bit of blade and decided
to classify it as a knife, he could get ten days in the cells.

But a little knife for mending boots meant earning,
which meant bread!

It would be a pity to throw it away.

And Shukhov slipped it into one of his mittens.

Then the next row of five was ordered to go forward
to be searched.

And only three of them were left standing under the
bright lights: Senka, Shukhov and the young man from
Gang 32 who'd helped look for the Moldavian.

Because there were three of them and the guards facing them numbered five, Shukhov was able to weigh
up the two guards on the right, and choose which of the
two he would approach. He decided against the young,
red-faced one, and in favour of an older man with a
grey moustache. The old one was, of course, experienced and would easily be able to find the piece of blade
if he wanted to, but because he was old he must have
become so fed up with the job that it would be hateful
to him.

Meanwhile, Shukhov had taken off both mittens, the
one with the piece of blade and the empty one, and held
them in one hand (the empty one a little further forward)
along with the rope belt. He opened his jacket wide and
pushed back the skirts of his coat and jacket (never before had he been so obliging when preparing to be
searched, but this time he wanted to show that he was
"clean" – come on, then, search me!) – and on the com-

mand he moved towards the old man with the grey moustache.

The old man slapped Shukhov's sides and back and the outside of his knee pocket – nothing. He squeezed in his hands the skirts of Shukhov's jacket and coat – again, nothing. Just as he was on the point of letting him through, to be on the safe side he put his hand round the mitten which Shukov held out – the empty one.

The warder squeezed the mitten, and Shukhov felt as if his heart were being squeezed as well. One such squeeze on the other mitten, and he'd be in the cells on 300 grams of bread a day and hot food once every three days. He imagined at that moment how enfeebled and hungry he would become and how difficult it would be to recover his present condition of being neither starved nor properly fed.

And the vital prayer surged up within him: "Oh, Lord, save me! Don't let me be put in the cells!"

All these thoughts passed through him while the warder squeezed the first mitten and reached out his hand to squeeze the one behind it (he would have squeezed them one in each hand if Shukhov had held them in separate hands and not both in the same hand). But at that moment was heard the voice of the warder in charge of searching, anxious to be free as quickly as possible, shouting to the guards:

"Come on, bring up the men from the machine factory!"

And, instead of taking Shukhov's other mitten, the old warder with the grey moustache waved him through. Shukhov was off the hook.

He ran to catch up the others. They had already formed up in fives between two long wooden rails of the sort to which horses are hitched in market-places, and which made a kind of paddock for the column. He ran lightly, scarcely feeling the ground, but he didn't say a prayer of thanksgiving, because he didn't have time, and because in any case it didn't seem appropriate.

117

The escort guards who had brought the column in now moved to one side, freeing the way for the escort guards attached to the column from the machine factory, and they were now waiting for their chief. They had picked up all the firewood thrown down by the column before being searched, and the firewood which had been taken by the warders searching had been collected in a pile by the guard-room.

The moon was rising higher all the time, and the cold growing more intense in the bright, snowy night.

The Chief Escort Guard walked to the guard-room to get a receipt there for the 463 men he had delivered. He spoke to Pryakha Volkovoi's assistant, and then shouted:

"K–460!"

The Moldavian, who had been hiding himself in the middle of the column, sighed and went up to the rail on the right. He was still hanging his head low and his shoulders were hunched up.

"Come here," Pryakha said, indicating to him to walk to the other side of the column.

The Moldavian walked round. He was ordered to put his hands behind his back and stand there.

It meant that they were going to get him for attempting to escape. He'd go to the cells, all right.

Just in front of the gates, to the right and left of the paddock, stood two guards. The gates, which were three times the height of a man, were slowly opened, and the command was given:

"Line up in fives!" (There was no point in ordering the prisoners to stand back from the gates here, since all the gates into the camp opened inwards, and the prisoners would get nowhere should they attempt to break through the gates from the inside.) "One! Two! Three!"

It was at this evening count, when they returned through the camp gates, that the prisoners felt most weather-beaten, cold and hungry – and their bowl of thin, hotted-up cabbage soup in the evening was, for

118

them, like rain in a drought. They swallowed it in one gulp. That bowl of soup was more precious to them than freedom, more precious than their previous life and the life which the future held for them.

They passed through the camp gates, those prisoners, like soldiers returning from a campaign – keyed up, seasoned, bold. "Watch out, we're coming," they seemed to say.

For an orderly who'd spent the day in the staff barracks, that surge of returning prisoners must have been a frightening sight.

After the evening count, the prisoners became free men for the first time since being called on parade in the morning. They passed through the big camp gates, through some smaller gates further on, through a couple more barriers to the parade ground – where the column dispersed, and they could go where they wanted.

Except, that is, for the gang-leaders, who were summoned by a warder:

"Gang-leaders! Report to the PPD!"

Shukhov ran past the prison block, between the barracks – to the parcels' office; and Tsesar moved in a leisurely and regular way in the opposite direction, where a number of people were swarming around a post with a plywood board nailed to it on which was written in pencil the names of those who had received parcels that day.

They rarely used paper in the camp – usually plywood. It was stronger, certainly, and somehow more trustworthy than paper. It was used by the guards and counters for counting the prisoners. They could wipe it clean for the next day and use it again – a great economy.

There was a queue around the walls of the vestibule which formed the entrance to the parcels' office. Shukhov joined it. There were fifteen or so men in front of him, which meant that he would have to wait at least an hour – or until lights out. But if anybody from his, the power station column – or from the machine factory column – had been to see if his name was on the board, he would certainly be behind Shukhov in the queue. And he would probably have to come back to get his parcel another time – tomorrow morning.

The men stood in the queue with little bags and sacks. There, on the other side of the door (Shukhov had never once received a parcel in this camp, but he knew from hearsay), they would open up the box in which the parcel came with a small axe, and the warder would take everything out with his hands and inspect it carefully. He would cut anything, break anything, handle anything, mix anything. If there was anything liquid, in glass jars or tins, they'd open it up and pour it out for you – either straight into your hands, or into a cloth bag if you were carrying one. They didn't give you the jars or cans, they were scared to. If there was anything made of pastry, or something sweet, or any sausage or fish, then the warder would take a bite out of it. (And if you started to object, he'd immediately say that the stuff was forbidden or wasn't regulation, and wouldn't give it to you anyway. Anyone receiving a parcel had to give, give, give all along the line – starting with the warder who opened it.) And when they'd finished searching through your parcel, they didn't give you the box in which the stuff came, you just had to shove it all into your bag or even into the skirts of your coat. And off you went, and it was the next fellow's turn. They harried you so much that you sometimes left something behind on the counter. There was no point going back for this: it would have gone.

When he'd been at Ust-Izhma, Shukhov had received a couple of parcels. But he'd written to his wife that it was just a waste and not to send them – better not deprive the children.

Although it had been easier for Shukhov, when he was free, to feed his whole family than it was here to feed only himself, he knew what these gift-parcels cost,

120

and he knew that he couldn't go on taking the food out of the mouths of his family for ten years. Better that he should do without.

But although that was what he had decided, every time someone in the gang or near to him in the barracks received a parcel (and that was nearly every day), his heart ached that the parcel wasn't for him. And though he had expressly told his wife never to send a parcel, even at Easter, and he never went to the post with the list of recipients on it except on behalf of some rich member of his gang – yet sometimes he longed for somebody to run up to him and say:

"Shukhov! Why don't you get going? There's a parcel for you."

But nobody ever ran up to him . . .

And there were fewer and fewer occasions to recall the village of Temgenovo and the hut where he and his family lived . . . Here life pursued him from reveille to lights out, and there was no free time available for reminiscing.

Now, standing among men dwelling on the near prospect of sinking their teeth into a lump of lard, being able to spread their bread with butter and to sweeten their mugs of tea with sugar, Shukhov had only one wish: to be in time, with his gang, to get to the mess-hall, and to be able to eat his gruel before it had got cold. Cold, it was only half as satisfying as when it was hot.

He reckoned that if Tsesar's name had not appeared on the list, he would long ago have gone to the barracks to clean up. But if his name was on the list, he'd now be getting together bags and plastic mugs to hold the contents of his parcel. That's why Shukhov had promised to wait for ten minutes.

There, in the queue, Shukhov learned some news: there wasn't going to be any Sunday again this week – they were going to be deprived of another Sunday. He'd been expecting it, and they all had: if there were five Sundays in a month, they got three free and had to work

121

on the other two. He'd been expecting it, but when he heard the news, his whole spirits sank, and it was like being hit in the face: how could you not resent the loss of that day? But what they were saying in the queue was right: even if it was a free Sunday, they'd find something for you to do in the camp, invent something – fixing up the bath-house, putting up a new wall to prevent you getting somewhere, cleaning out the yard. Or there'd be mattresses to be changed and shaken, bedbugs to be exterminated. Or they'd devise a parade for checking photographs against people's faces. Or there'd be an inventory: you'd have to move all your things out into the yard, and spend half the day sitting about.

The one thing they couldn't stand, for sure, was a prisoner having a sleep after breakfast.

The queue was moving, although slowly. Three people – a camp barber, a bookkeeper and someone from the CES – broke the queue and pushed up front, elbowing their way through without so much as a word to anyone. But these weren't regular prisoners but established camp trusties, bastards of the first water with soft numbers in the camp. These people were regarded by the workers as lower than shit (a feeling that was reciprocated). But it would have been useless to argue with them: they kept close together and were well in with the warders.

Now there were only ten people ahead of Shukhov – and seven more had joined the queue behind him when Tsesar appeared in the door and, stooping, came through, wearing a new fur cap which had been sent from home. (That cap, now. Tsesar must have greased somebody's palm to be allowed to go around in that clean, new town cap. Others had had their frayed army caps taken from them as soon as they entered the camp, and been issued with regulation pig-fur caps.)

Tsesar smiled at Shukhov and immediately began talking to an odd-looking fellow in glasses, who was standing in the queue reading a newspaper:

"Aha, Pyotr Mikhailitch!"

And they blossomed out like a couple of poppies.

"Look!" The odd-looking fellow said. "I've just got a fresh *Evening News* from Moscow! It came by newspaper post."

"Well, well!" And Shukhov poked his nose into the newspaper. How on earth could they decipher that small print in the meagre light cast by the lamp on the ceiling?

"Here's an extremely interesting review of a Zavadsky first night . . ."

These Muscovites can smell each other from a long way off, like dogs. And when they come together, they sniff away at each other. And they jabber away very, very fast, each trying to say more words than the other. And when they jabber away like that, you rarely seem to hear any proper Russian words – they might just as well be Latvians or Rumanians.

However, Tsesar had all his little bags in his hand, everything ready.

"So I . . . Tsesar Markovitch . . ." Shukhov lisped. "I'll be going now, all right?"

"Of course, of course." Tsesar raised his black moustache from the paper. "But, tell me, who am I after, and who's after me?"

Shukhov told him where his place was in the queue, and not waiting for Tsesar himself to remember the subject of supper, he asked:

"And shall I bring you your supper?"

(That meant from the mess-hall to the barracks in a can. This was emphatically forbidden, and there were many orders concerning the practice. If you got caught, they emptied the can onto the ground and shoved you in the cells. Nevertheless, people went on carrying food in this way, and would continue to do so, because if someone had anything to do, he would never have time to get to the mess-hall with the rest of the gang.)

When Shukhov asked: "And shall I bring you your

supper?" he thought to himself: "You're not going to be so mean, are you as not to let me have your supper? You know there's no porridge for supper, only thin gruel!"

"No, no," smiled Tsesar. "Eat it yourself, Ivan Denisovitch!"

That was all that Shukhov had been waiting for! Now, like a bird on the wing, he rushed out through the vestibule – and across the parade ground.

There were prisoners scurrying about all over the place! At one time the camp Commandant had issued an order that no prisoner was to walk alone about the camp. Wherever possible, the gang had to go all together – except to places like the infirmary or the latrines, when the whole gang couldn't obviously go at the same time; but, in those events, groups of four or five men were to be made up, one of them to be in charge to march them where they wanted to go, wait, and then march them back in a single body.

The camp Commandant had been very firm about this order, and nobody had dared to oppose him. The warders seized prisoners walking on their own, recorded their numbers, and shoved them in the cells. But the order collapsed – quietly and gradually like many high-sounding orders had a habit of doing. Say someone was summoned by the security people – did he have to go in a group of other people? Or if you had to get something from the stores – "Why should I go along with you?" And if someone had the idea of going to the CES to read the newspapers, who would he get to go with him? And this man wants to get his felt boots repaired, that man to go to the drying-room, this man simply to go from one barracks to another (although that was forbidden above everything else!) – well, how can you prevent them?

With his order, the Commandant had wanted to take away from the prisoners the last vestiges of freedom they possessed, but it didn't work out like that, the pot-bellied old fool.

On his way back to the barracks, Shukhov ran into a warder, took his cap off to him to be on the safe side, and made it to the barracks. Inside the barracks was pandemonium: somebody's bread ration had been stolen during the day, and the fellow was shouting at the orderlies and the orderlies were shouting at him. The corner which Gang 104 occupied was empty.

Shukhov always reckoned they'd been lucky, when they returned to the camp in the evening, if the mattresses hadn't been messed up and the barracks searched during the day.

He dashed over to his bunk, slipping his coat off his shoulders as he went. He threw the coat up onto his bunk, together with his mittens and, still inside one, the bit of blade, and felt inside his mattress – the bread was still there! A good thing that he'd sewn it in.

And he ran outside again – to the mess-hall.

He got there without coming across a single warder – only a couple of prisoners quarrelling over their bread ration.

Outside the moon was shining ever more brightly. The lamps everywhere looked pale, and the barracks cast black shadows. The entrance to the mess-hall was through a wide porch with four steps, and the porch was in the shadows too. Above it a small lamp swayed and creaked in the cold. And all the lamps shone with a kind of rainbow effect, whether caused by the cold or simply dirt he didn't know.

And there was another order the camp Commandant was particularly keen on: members of a gang should proceed into the mess-hall in twos. And an extension of the order was that, having reached the mess-hall, the gang was not to proceed through the porch, but form up in fives outside and wait there until allowed into the mess-hall by the orderly.

Khromoi* hung on fiercely to his job as mess-hall

*Khromoi means lame in Russian

125

orderly. With his limp he was able to pass himself off as an invalid, although he was perfectly strong, the vulture. He'd got himself a staff made out of birch and, standing at the top of the porch, would let anybody who tried to creep by him without his permission have it with this staff. Well, not anybody. Khromoi had eyes like a lynx and could spot you in the dark from behind – and he'd only hit out when he knew that person wouldn't hit back. He'd only go for those who felt beaten already. He'd caught Shukhov a blow once.

He was called an orderly, but when you thought about it, he was a prince – friendly with the cooks and all!

Today the gangs must have all poured into the mess-hall at the same time, or it had taken longer than usual to get things organised inside, because the porch was thick with people, and on the porch stood Khromoi and his assistant and the head of the mess-hall himself. They were trying to keep things in order without warders, the tough guys.

The head of the mess-hall was a fat swine with a head like a pumpkin and shoulders a yard wide. He was so over-endowed with strength that when he walked he used to spring up and down as if his legs and arms were, indeed, made of springs. He wore a white cap made of soft fur without a number on it, and it was of a quality not seen in ordinary, outside life. He wore a lambskin waistcoat with a number on it in the front the size of a postage stamp – a concession to Volkovoi – and no number on the back at all. He bowed to nobody, and all the prisoners were scared of him. He held a thousand lives in his hands. Once they'd tried to beat him up, but all the cooks had rushed to his defence – and an ugly bunch of mugs they were.

Shukhov would be in trouble if Gang 104 had already gone in. Khromoi knew everybody in the camp by sight, and in front of the head of the mess-hall he would never let anyone through who wasn't with his gang – in fact, would make a point of tearing a strip off him.

Sometimes prisoners had managed to climb over the porch railings behind Khromoi's back. Shukhov had done this, too. But today you couldn't try this on with the head of the mess-hall present – he'd give you such a crack that you'd only just be able to drag yourself to the infirmary.

He'd have to make it over to the porch as quickly as possible, and see if, among all those black coats which looked identical in the dark, Gang 104 was there.

Just as he got there, the gangs began shoving and shoving (what else was there for them to do – it was nearly lights out!) as if storming a fortress. They got up the first step, the second, the third, the fourth – they spilled into the porch!

"Stop, you bastards!" Khromoi yelled and raised his stick at the men in front. "Get back! Or I'll smash your faces in!"

"What can we do?" the men in front shouted back. "We're being pushed from behind!"

And, indeed, it was true, the pushing did come from behind, but the men in front didn't put up any resistance, anxious as they were to break into the mess-hall.

Then Khromoi put his staff across his chest as a kind of barrier and charged at the men in front with all his might! And Khromoi's assistant got hold of the stick as well and pushed, and the head of the mess-hall seemed ready to soil his hands in addition . . .

They pushed with all their strength – and they had plenty of it with all that meat they filled themselves with! The men in front were pushed back onto those behind them, who fell against those behind them, and they went down like sheaves.

"Fuck you, Khromoi!" shouted somebody from the crowd, but he was well hidden. The rest fell down without a word, picked themselves up without a word, as quickly as they could before they got trampled.

The steps cleared. The head of the mess-hall went

back inside, but Khromoi stood on the top step and shouted:

"Line up in fives, you blockheads, how many times have you been told? I'll let you through when we're ready for you!"

Shukhov thought he saw what could have been Senka Klevshin's head right by the porch. He felt quite over-joyed and started trying to push his way through with his elbows. But the backs in front of him drew together, and he knew he didn't have the strength to make it.

"Gang 27!" Khromoi shouted. "Forward!"

Gang 27 leapt forward up the steps towards the doors as quickly as possible. Everybody else surged up the steps again after them, the men at the back pushing hard. Shukhov also pushed for all he was worth. The porch shook, and the lamp above the porch squeaked.

"So you're doing it again, you bastards!" Khromoi was furious. He brought his stick down across one man's shoulders, somebody else's back, shoving them back against the others.

From below Shukhov could see Pavlo moving up the steps towards Khromoi. He was in charge of the gang. Tyurin didn't care to get mixed up in this sort of crush.

"Line up in fives, Gang 104!" Pavlo shouted from the top. "Let them through, friends!"

Friends, indeed! The hell they'd let them through!

"Hey, let me through, you! That's my gang!" Shukhov shoved against the man in front of him.

The man would have been glad to let him through, but he was jammed in on every side.

The crowd rocked from side to side – ready to do anything to get their gruel, their lawful gruel.

Then Shukhov tried something different. He seized hold of the rails on his left, grabbed one of the posts in the porch and pulled himself off the ground. His feet hit somebody on the knee, he got bashed in the ribs him-self and picked up a few oaths – but he got through. He stood with one foot on the edge of the top step and waited. Some of the men from his gang saw him and stretched out their hands to him.

The head of the mess-hall came out and looked around:

"Come on, Khromoi, let's have another two gangs."

"Gang 104!" Khromoi shouted. "And where do you think you're going, you bastard?"

And he caught the intruder a blow on the neck with his staff.

"Gang 104!" Pavlo shouted, letting his men through.

"Phew!" Shukhov entered the mess-hall, exhausted. But without waiting for Pavlo to ask him, he began looking around for empty trays.

The mess-hall was as usual – clouds of steam coming through the door, the men packed tightly against each other at the tables, like the seeds of a sunflower, or wandering around and pushing each other between the tables, looking for empty trays. But Shukhov had got used to all this over the years. He had a sharp eye, and he saw that S-208 was carrying a tray with only five bowls on it – which meant that it was the last load for his gang, because otherwise the tray would have been fully loaded.

He went up to the man and said in his ear from behind:

"After you with the tray, brother!"

"There's another fellow at the hatch waiting for it, I promised him ..."

"Let him wait, he should have been quicker!"

And they reached an agreement.

The man carried the tray over to his table and unloaded it, and Shukhov immediately seized hold of it. The man to whom it had been promised came running over and grabbed the other end of the tray. But he was smaller than Shukhov, so Shukhov pushed him away with the tray so that he hurtled against one of the pillars in the mess-hall, and his hands let go, Shukhov put the tray under his arm and dashed over to the hatch.

Pavlo was standing in the queue by the hatch, concerned that he had no trays. He was delighted to see Shukhov:

"Ivan Denisovitch!" And he pushed the second-in-command of Gang 27, who was standing in front of him, out of the way. "Let me through! What are you standing there for? I've got some trays!"

He could see that Gopchik, the little rascal, was carrying a tray over as well.

"They were too slow," he laughed, "and I just grabbed it!"

Gopchik was going to do all right in the camp. Give him another three years to grow up in, and he'd be not less than a bread-cutter, it was inevitable.

Pavlo ordered that the second tray should be taken by Yermolayev, a big Siberian who'd got ten years for being captured by the Germans. And Gopchik was sent to keep an eye out for a table which would shortly become free. Shukhov put down his tray in the hatch and waited.

"Gang 104!" Pavlo shouted through the hatch.

There were five such hatches: three serving hatches for ordinary food, one for those who got special food (there were ten men who suffered from ulcers; and the bookkeepers had managed to get themselves in on this special food), and one for the return of the bowls (where the bowl-lickers would congregate and squabble with each other). The hatches weren't very high – scarcely waist height. You couldn't see the cooks themselves through the hatches, only their hands and the ladles.

The cook's hands were white and carefully tended, but they were big and hairy. More like a boxer's hands than a cook's. He took up a pencil and checked a list on the wall:

"Gang 104! Twenty-four bowls!"

Pantaleyev dragged himself into the mess-hall. Nothing wrong with him, the swine.

The cook picked up an enormous ladle and stirred the mess in the cauldron – three times. The cauldron had just been refilled, nearly to the top, and billows of steam were rising from it. Then, swapping the big ladle for a smaller one, he began to serve, not letting his ladle go deep into the cauldron.

"One, two, three, four . . ."

Shukhov noticed that some of the bowls had been filled before the bits in the gruel had had time to settle back on the bottom of the cauldron, that others had no substance in them at all – just wash. He put ten bowls on his tray and carried it off. Gopchik waved at him from the second row of pillars:

"Here, Ivan Denisovitch, here!"

You had to be careful not to let your hands shake carrying these bowls. Shukhov walked as smoothly as he could, so as not to jolt the tray in any way, and worked as hard with his throat:

"Hey, you, H–920, watch what you're doing . . . Out of my way, uncle . . . Step aside, lad . . ."

It was difficult enough in a crush like this to carry one bowl without spilling it, but to carry ten. Nevertheless, he put the tray down gently on the free end of the table which Gopchik had found, and not a drop had he spilled. And he so arranged it that the two bowls most full of substance were at that end of the tray opposite to where he was going to sit himself.

Yermolayev brought another ten bowls over. And Gopchik ran across to help Pavlo bring the last four bowls over by hand.

Kilgas brought the bread on a tray. Today they were being fed according to the work they had done – some got 200 grams, some 300, some 400. Shukhov got 400, which he took from the crust – and, from the middle, he took the 200 which Tsesar had earned.

Now the other members of the gang began to stream up from all parts of the mess-hall to get their supper and to eat it where they could. Shukhov handed out the bowls, remembering to whom he had given a bowl, and keeping an eye on his corner of the tray. He put his spoon into one of the "thick" bowls – which meant that it had been taken. Fetyukov was one of the first to collect his bowl, and he then went off, reckoning that there was nothing to be cadged from his own gang, and that it would be better to parade round the mess-hall on the scrounge. Perhaps somebody would not finish his bowl (when that happened, a whole group of men would swoop on it like vultures, sometimes all at the same time).

Shukhov counted up the bowls with Pavlo, and everything seemed to be in order. He handed over one of the "thick" bowls for Tyurin, and Pavlo poured the contents into a little mess-tin with a lid – he could carry that under his coat, pressed to his chest.

The trays were given up. Pavlo sat down to his double portion, and so did Shukhov. They didn't talk to each other, these minutes were holy.

Shukhov took off his cap and rested it on his knee. He put his spoon into one bowl and tasted, and then did the same with the other. Not bad, and there was some fish. In general, the gruel in the evening was much more watery than in the morning: in the morning, the prisoners had to eat in order to work, in the evening, all they had to do was go to sleep.

He began to eat. First of all, he drank just the watery stuff at the top. As it went down, the warmth flooded through his whole body – and his insides seemed to be quivering in expectation of that gruel. Goo-ood! It was for this brief moment that a prisoner lived!

And now Shukhov had no complaints – about the length of his sentence, about the long day they had had, about the Sunday they would not be having. Now he thought: "We'll survive! We'll get through it all! God grant that it'll end!"

He drank the hot wash from both bowls, then poured the remaining contents of the second bowl into the first, scraping it clean with his spoon. It was easier that way. He didn't have to think about the second bowl, keep watching over it with his eyes or a hand.

His eyes were free to look around now, and he glanced at the bowls near him. The man on his left – his bowl was just water. They were swines what they'd do, and they were prisoners as well!

Shukhov began to eat the cabbage in what was left of his gruel. He came across a small piece of potato in one of the two bowls – Tsesar's bowl. An average sort of piece, frostbitten of course, and somewhat hard and sweet. But there was very little fish – an occasional bit of bare backbone. But you had to suck away at every bit of backbone or fin – to get the juice out of it, for the juice was nutritious. All this took time, of course, but Shukhov was in no hurry now. Today had been a good day: he'd got an extra portion at dinner, and an extra portion now as well. In view of that, he could forget about everything else he might have done.

Although he ought really to pay a visit to the Latvian for some tobacco. There might not be any left by tomorrow.

Shukhov ate his supper without bread – two portions and bread as well would have been too much! So he kept his bread for the next day. Your belly is a cruel master – however well you've treated it one day, it'll be singing for more the next.

Shukhov finished up his gruel without making any effort to see who was sitting around him. It hadn't been necessary: he'd had a good whack himself, and hadn't been on the lookout for anything on top. All the same, he noticed that, when the man directly opposite him vacated his place, a tall, old man – U–81 – sat himself down. He was, he knew, from Gang 64, and Shukhov had heard when waiting in the parcels' queue that it was Gang 64 who had been sent that day to work at the Socialist Community Centre instead of Gang 104. They'd been out there all day, without any kind of shelter, putting up barbed wire – to fence themselves in with.

Shukhov had been told that this old man had spent

133

countless years in camps and prisons, and had never benefited from a single amnesty, and that whenever one ten-year sentence ran out, then they slapped another one on him immediately. Now Shukhov examined him closely. Among all those men in the camp with bent backs, his back stood out as straight as a board, and it seemed as if he had put something on the bench beneath him to lift himself up. For a long time there had been nothing to shave off his bare head – he had lost all his hair as a result of the good life, no doubt! The old man's eyes didn't dart around to see what was going on in the mess-hall, but were fixed above Shukhov's head at some invisible spot of his own. He ate the thin gruel with a worn wooden spoon at his own pace, but he didn't bend his head towards the spoon – but carried the spoon all the way to his mouth. He had no teeth at all in his upper gums, and not one in the lower half of his mouth either, and he used his hardened gums as teeth to chew his bread. His face was quite drained of life, but did not look weak or unhealthy – rather, looked dark and as if hewn out of stone. And from his hands, which were big and cracked and blackened, you could see that not much soft work had come his way in all those years. But it was clear that the one thing he wasn't going to do was give in: he wasn't going to put his bread, like everybody else, straight down on the filthy table – but on a piece of cloth which had obviously been washed many times.

However, Shukhov had no time to go on looking at the man. Having finished eating, he licked his spoon and shoved it into the top of his felt boot, pulled his cap over his eyes, stood up, took his own and Tsesar's bread ration, and went out. The way out of the mess-hall was through another porch, where stood a couple of orderlies, whose only job it was to unhook the door, let people through, then put the hook on the door again.

Shukhov came out with a full belly, feeling pleased with himself, and he decided that, although lights out was pretty imminent, he would run over to see the Latvian. Without stopping off at Barrack 9, his own, to leave his bread there, he strode off in the direction of Barracks 7.

The moon was right up high now and looked as if cut out of the sky – clean and white. The sky was completely clear, and the stars were at their brightest. But Shukhov had even less time for gazing at the sky. One thing he did realise – the frost hadn't let up. Someone had heard one of the outside workers say that it would be – 30 in the night and – 40 by morning.

He could hear the noise of a tractor in the distance – working in the settlement outside the camp, and from the direction of the highway the screaming of an excavator. And from every pair of felt boots on the move throughout the camp – crunch, crunch.

There was no wind.

Shukhov would have to buy the tobacco for the price he'd paid before – one rouble per mug; although, outside, such a mugful would cost three roubles – more for better quality tobacco. But in the camp all prices were of their own devising, and were not comparable to anywhere else, because in the camp you weren't supposed to have money, and it was very difficult to get hold of. In a punishment camp like this one, you weren't paid a single copeck for the work you did (at Ust-Izhma Shukhov used to get thirty roubles a month). And if you received any money through the post from relations, you didn't actually get that money, but it was marked up in a personal account. And every month you could buy with money in your personal account stuff at the camp-store – soap, mouldy biscuits, "Prima" cigarettes. Whether you liked what you got or not, you had to spend what you had applied to the Commandant to spend. If you didn't buy anything with the money, they'd have taken it out of your personal account all the same.

Shukhov got money only by doing odd jobs – making slippers out of rags given to him by the buyer (two roubles), patching a jacket (by negotiation).

Barracks 7, unlike Barracks 9, was not made up of two big halves. There was a long corridor, with ten doors opening off it, and behind each door a room which housed a complete gang, packed into seven tiered bunks. And there was a latrine to each room, and a cabin for the man in charge of the barracks. The artists had a cabin to themselves as well.

Shukhov went to the room where the Latvian was. The Latvian was lying on a lower bunk, his feet up on a ledge. He was chattering away to a neighbour in Latvian.

Shukhov sat down beside him, and greeted him. The Latvian returned his greeting without taking his feet down. It was a small room, and everyone was keeping his ears open – who is this fellow? Why has he come? They both realised that, and that's why Shukhov sat there talking about nothing special. Well, and how's life? Not bad. Cold today. Yes.

Shukhov waited for everybody to begin talking again (they were arguing about the Korean War; whether, now the Chinese had entered the war, there would be a world war or not), then leaned towards the Latvian and said:

"Any home-grown?"

"Yes."

"Show it me."

The Latvian lowered his feet from the ledge, dropped them on the floor, and sat up. He was a real skinflint, that Latvian, and when he filled a mug with tobacco, he would shake with fear that he had given you one smoke too many.

He showed Shukhov his pouch and unfastened it.

Shukhov took a few strands of tobacco and put them on his palm. It looked the same as last time, brownish and strong-flavoured. He held it to his nose and sniffed. Yes, that was it. But to the Latvian he said:

"It doesn't seem to be the same."

"Of course it's the same!" the Latvian answered angrily. "I never have any other, it's always the same."

"All right," agreed Shukhov. "Pack the mug for me,

136

I'll have a smoke, and maybe I'll have another mug-ful."

He had used the word "pack", because the Latvian always tried to fill the mug up loosely.

The Latvian reached under his pillow for another pouch, fuller than the first, and took a little mug out of a locker. Although the mug was made of plastic, Shukhov knew just how much it would hold, and that it was as good as glass for his purposes.

The Latvian began to fill the mug.

"Press it down, press it down!" Shukhov said, and poked his finger in.

"I know, I know," the Latvian retorted angrily, pulling the mug away and pressing down on the tobacco himself, although gently. And he continued to fill it.

Meanwhile Shukhov opened his jacket and found the place inside the padding where he had hidden – in such a way that nobody else could find it – his two-rouble note. With both his hands he forced it through the padding, and got it along to a little hole in a different spot which he'd torn and then sewn up with a couple of stitches. He tore open the hole with his nails, folded the note lengthways (it had already been folded this way before), and pulled it through the whole. Two roubles. Old note which didn't crackle.

There was shouting in the room:

"Do you think that old so-and-so with a moustache* is going to have any mercy on you? He wouldn't lift a finger for his own brother, let alone you, you creep!"

There was one good thing about a punishment camp – you were free to let off steam. At Ust-Izhma, if you'd said even in a whisper that you couldn't buy matches outside, they'd shove you in the cells and add another ten years to your sentence. But here you could shout your head off if you wanted – the squealers wouldn't tell on you, and the security people couldn't care less.

If only there had been more time in which to talk . . .

* Stalin

137

"Hey, you're putting it in loose," Shukhov complained.

"All right, all right!" the Latvian said, and added a few strands of tobacco on top.

Shukhov took his pouch from his inside pocket and poured the tobacco in from the mug.

"O.K.," he decided, not wishing to smoke that first sweet cigarette in a hurry. "Give me a second mugful."

He haggled a bit more with the Latvian, emptied the second mug into his pouch, handed over the two roubles, nodded and left.

Outside again, he hurried to get back to his barracks. He didn't want to miss Tsesar when he got back with his parcel.

But Tsesar was already there, sitting on his lower bunk and gloating over his parcel. He had laid out everything he had received on his bunk and on the locker, but as the light did not fall directly there – Shukhov's bunk above was in the way – it was all rather dark.

Shukhov bent down, stepped between the captain's bunk and Tsesar's, and stretched out his hand with the bread ration.

"Your bread, Tsesar Markovitch."

He didn't say: "Well, did you get your parcel?" That would have been to say, well, I kept a place in the queue for you, and now I have a right to a share. But Shukhov wasn't a cadger even after eight years in punishment camps – and the more time that went by, the more resolute he became about this.

However, he couldn't help revealing himself with his eyes. His eyes, the hawk-eyes of an experienced prisoner, ran rapidly over the contents of the parcel laid out on the bunk and locker, and although the paper had not been unwrapped and the little bags were as yet untied, in that one swift look and from the evidence of his nose, Shukhov knew for certain that Tsesar had received sausage, condensed milk, a fat smoked fish, lard, two kinds of biscuits, two kilograms of lump sugar, and also some butter, cigarettes and pipe tobacco. And there was more besides.

Shukhov took all this in in the short time it took him to say:

"Your bread, Tsesar Markovitch."

But Tsesar, who was in a state of high excitement and seemed almost drunk (people getting parcels always got into this sort of condition), waved the bread away:

"Take it, Ivan Denisovitch!"

Tsesar's bowl of gruel and now 200 grams of bread – that was a full supper and, of course, Shukhov's fair share of Tsesar's parcel.

And Shukhov immediately dismissed from his mind the idea that he might have got something good from what Tsesar had laid out all around him. There was nothing worse than exciting your belly to no purpose.

Well, he had 400 grams now, and Tsesar's 200, and at least 200 in his mattress. That was doing all right. He'd eat 200 now, tomorrow morning he'd get another 550, and he could take 400 to work – living it up, eh! And he'd leave that bit in the mattress. A good thing that he'd sewn it in. Someone from Gang 75 had had his ration pinched from the locker – and a fat lot he could do about it now.

Some people used to think that a parcel immediately solved for all time all the problems of the fellow who received it. There it was, a big, tightly-packed bag just waiting to be opened. But when you thought about it, it didn't take long to get through it. More frequently than not, before he got his parcel, a prisoner would be only too glad to earn himself an extra bowl of porridge some-how – and smoke other people's dog-ends. And there was the warder and the gang-leader to think of – and how could you avoid giving something to the orderly in the parcels' office? The next time the orderly might de-cide to "lose" your parcel for a while, and your name wouldn't appear on the list for a week. And there was the man in the store-room, to whom you handed your stuff for safe-keeping – and Tsesar would be going along there tomorrow before parade with his little bag – against thieves and searchers and by order of the Commandant, he had to get his whack, and a good one, if you didn't want him nibbling his way through your stuff. He sat there all day, the rat, with other people's food, how could you check up on him? And then there were those who had been of service to you, like Shukhov. And if the orderly in the bathhouse was going to give you a decent set of underwear, then there was a little something you had to give him. And the barber – not much perhaps, but three or four cigarettes to him if he was going to wipe the razor on a bit of paper, and not on your bare knee. And the people at the CES for keeping your letters separate, and not losing them. And if you wanted to lie on your back for a day or so in camp – there was the doctor to pay off. And your neighbour, with whom you shared a locker, in Tsesar's case the captain – you couldn't not give him something. He saw every bit you had, and you'd be a hard man not to let him have something.

There were some people who always thought the radish in the other fellow's hand was bigger and better – let them be the envious ones. But Shukhov understood life, and he didn't want to stretch his belly at anybody else's expense.

Meanwhile he took off his boots, climbed up to his bunk, drew the bit of hacksaw blade from his mitten, inspected it and decided that tomorrow he would look around for a good stone on which to grind it down to make a knife for mending shoes. It would take him about four days, if he worked away morning and night, and then he'd have a perfect little knife with a sharp, curved blade.

But now he had to hide the bit of blade, if only until morning. He'd push it into the gap under the cross-beam of his bunk. And while the captain was still not in his bunk below – he didn't want any rubbish to fall onto the captain's face — Shukhov turned back the corner of his heavy mattress, which was stuffed with saw-dust and not wood-shavings, and began to conceal the bit of blade.

His neighbours on the top were able to see him: Alyoshka the Baptist and, across the way, the two Estonians. But Shukhov had nothing to fear from them.

Fetyukov came into the barracks, sobbing. He was hunched up, and there was blood all over his lips. He must have been beaten up again for cadging from other people's bowls. Without looking at anyone, and without attempting to conceal his tears, he passed by the entire gang, climbed up to his bunk and buried his face in his mattress.

It was a shame really, when you thought about it. He would not survive his sentence. He just didn't know how to cope.

Then the captain came in, looking cheerful, and carrying a pot of special tea. Two wooden tea-urns stood in the barracks, but the tea that came out of them ... It was more or less hot and the right colour, but it was like dishwater, and smelled of rotten, saturated wood. This tea was for the lowest of the low. But the captain must have got some real tea from Tsesar, have chucked it into a pot and run off to get some hot water. He looked thoroughly pleased with himself, and made himself comfortable beside the locker below.

"Nearly scalded my fingers under the tap!" he boasted.

Also below, Tsesar was spreading out some sheets of paper, and putting this and that on it. Shukhov turned his mattress back, he did not want to see and get disturbed by the sight of all that food. But again they couldn't manage without him — Tsesar stood up and, with his eyes level with Shukhov's, winked:

"Ivan Denisovitch! Lend me your 'ten days', will you?"

That meant Shukhov's small pen-knife — possession of which, if he were caught, would mean ten days in the cells. He also kept this under the cross-beam of his bunk. It measured no more than half his little finger, but the little rascal could cut through lard five fingers' thick. Shukhov had made the knife himself, had ground it and sharpened it all on his own.

He pushed his hand under the cross-beam, took out the knife and handed it to Tsesar – who nodded and disappeared from view.

You could earn good money with a knife like that – but it meant the cells all right if they found it on you. Only a man without any conscience at all would have said: "Here, lend me your knife, we're going to cut up some sausage" without feeling some sense of obligation.

So once more Tsesar was in Shukhov's debt.

The issues of the bread and the knives out of the way, Shukhov proceeded to pull out his tobacco-pouch. Then he took from it as much tobacco as he had earlier borrowed, and stretched across to the Estonian with it. Thanks.

The Estonian spread his lips, as if in a smile, and mumbled something to his neighbour, the other Estonian, and they rolled the tobacco Shukhov had given into a cigarette – to test its quality.

It was no worse than theirs, so go ahead and try it. Shukhov would have liked to try the stuff himself, but some sort of time-keeper inside his head told him that there wasn't much time before the evening check. Now was about the time that the warders would come barging around the barracks. He would have to go out into the corridor to have a smoke, but he felt quite warm up there on his bunk. In fact, the barracks was not at all warm, and frost still coated the ceiling. At the moment it was fairly tolerable, but they'd certainly freeze up during the night.

So Shukhov stayed on his bunk and began to break up the 200-gram piece of bread into pieces, listening against his will to the captain and Tsesar conversing below, while they drank their tea.

"Help yourself, captain, help yourself, don't hold back! Take some smoked fish, a bit of sausage."

"Thank you, I will."

"And spread some of that butter on your bread! It's real Moscow bread!"

"It's hard to believe that real bread is made any more. You know, all this profusion reminds me of the time when I happened to be in Archangel . . ."

There was so much noise from the two hundred voices in Shukhov's half of the barracks, that he wasn't sure if he heard the rail being banged or not. Nobody else seemed to have. He also noticed that Snub-nose, one of the warders, had come into the barracks – he was a tiny young man with a red face. He was holding a bit of paper in his hand, and it was evident from this and from the way he behaved that he hadn't come simply to catch illicit smokers or kick everybody out for the evening check, but that he was looking for somebody.

He confirmed something on the piece of paper and asked:

"Where's Gang 104?"

"Here," they answered him. And the Estonians hid their cigarette and waved away the smoke.

"Where's the gang-leader?"

"What do you want?" said Tyurin from his bunk, scarcely bothering to lower his legs to the floor.

"What about those reports by two of your men concerning extra clothing?"

"They're writing them," Tyurin answered confidently.

"They should've been in by now."

"The men haven't had much education, it is not easy for them." (This was about Tsesar and the captain. The gang-leader was sharp, never lost for a word.) "And there're no pens, no ink."

"They should have them."

"They've been taken away."

"Now, watch out, gang-leader, if you go on talking like that, I'll slap you in the cells!" Snub-nose promised

143

Tyurin, but not too angrily. "See that those reports get to the staff barracks tomorrow morning before parade! And give orders that all unofficial garments be surrendered at the store-room for personal property. Understood?"

"Understood."

("The captain's got off!" thought Shukhov. The captain himself hadn't heard a thing, so intent was he on his sausage and talking to Tsesar.)

But . . .

"Now," said the warder. "S–311 – is he one of yours?"

"I'll have to look at my list," the gang-leader stalled. "You can't expect me to remember all those damned numbers, can you?" (The gang-leader was dragging things out, hoping that the evening check would intervene and keep the captain out of the cells until the following morning.)

But the warder said: "Buinovsky – are you here?"

"What? Yes, I'm here!" the captain called out from under cover of Shukhov's bunk.

It's always the quickest louse that's first to get caught in the comb.

"You? Yes, that's right, S–311. Come on, then."

"Where to?"

"You know well enough."

The captain just sighed and gave a grunt. It must have been easier for him to take a squadron of destroyers out to a stormy sea on a dark night than to break off his friendly conversation for an icy cell.

"How many days?" he asked in a low voice.

"Ten. Come on, then, get a move on!"

At that moment the orderlies came in, shouting:

"Evening check! Evening check! All out!"

This meant that the warder whom they'd sent to make the check was already in the barracks.

The captain looked round – should he take his coat? But they'd only take it away from him, and leave him

144

with only his jacket. In that case, better go as he was. The captain had hoped that Volkovoi would forget (although Volkovoi never forgot a thing), and he wasn't properly prepared – hadn't hidden any tobacco for himself in his jacket. And to carry it in his hands would have been pointless – they'd find it immediately they searched him.

Nevertheless, while he was putting on his cap, Tsesar slipped him a couple of cigarettes.

"Well, good-bye, brothers," the captain said and nodded in a confused way to Gang 104. He followed the warder out.

A few voices shouted to him: "Keep cheerful", "Don't let them get you down". What could you say? Gang 104 knew the cells, they'd built them themselves: stone walls, cement floor, no windows, a stove lit only to melt the ice on the walls, thereby causing pools of water on the floor. You slept on bare boards, and if your teeth did not fall out from chattering, 300 grams of bread to eat a day – and gruel only on every third day.

Ten days! Ten days in the cells in this camp – if you survived them – meant that your health had been ruined for the rest of your life. T.B., and in and out of hospital until that was that.

Fifteen days – and you were a dead man!

While you're living in barracks, you thank God and try to keep out of trouble.

"Come on, out before I count three!" the man in charge of the barracks shouted. "Whoever's not out by the time I count three will have his number taken and reported."

The fellow in charge of the barracks was a real swine. There he was, locked in with all the rest of them in the barracks for the night, but he behaved like an official and was afraid of nobody. The opposite, in fact, everybody was afraid of him. He'd give you over to the warders or smash you in the face. He was classified as an invalid, because he'd lost a finger in a fight, but you could

145

tell from his face that he was a thug. In fact, that's what he was – with a criminal record – but among other things they hung Article 58/14 on him, and that's how he ended up in the camp.

And he really would take your number and report you – and that meant two days in the cells with work. So they didn't make it to the door slowly, but rushed towards it all at once, and the men on the top bunks leapt off like bears and hurtled towards that narrow door.

Shukhov, holding the cigarette he'd just rolled in his hand – he hadn't been able to overcome his craving for it – jumped nimbly down, shoved his feet into his felt boots and started to move off. But he felt sorry for Tsesar. It wasn't that he wanted to get anything else out of Tsesar, he felt genuinely sorry for him. He thought so much of himself, and yet he didn't really understand life: having received a parcel, he shouldn't have gloated over it like that, but taken it straight to the store-room as quickly as possible before the evening check. He could have eaten the stuff any time, but what was he going to do with it now? He could have taken it all out with him in a bag to the evening check – but he'd be the laughing-stock of five hundred men. He could leave it in the barracks – but there was a good chance that it would be whipped by the first man back to the barracks. (At Ust-Izhma, it was even more cruel: there, the criminals would get back from work before the others and clean out all the lockers.)

Shukhov saw that Tsesar did not know what to do. He was fussing around all over the place – but it was too late. He was shoving the sausage and lard down his front – at least he could take those things out to the check and save them.

Shukhov took pity on him and gave some advice:

"Sit here, Tsesar Markovitch, until the very last. Hide yourself back in the shadows, and sit there until everybody's gone. And when the warder and the orderlies come walking round the bunks, looking into all the corners, then come out and say you're not feeling well. I'll go out first and I'll be the first back. That's what to do."

And Shukhov ran off.

At first he shoved his way roughly through the crowd of people (protecting his rolled cigarette in his fist, however). In the corridor into which both halves of the barracks led and by the doorway, nobody was in a hurry to go forward; the crafty lot stuck close to the walls in two rows to the right and left – leaving passage down the middle of the corridor for only one man to get through. They didn't want to go out into the cold, and only a fool would if he could stay inside. They'd been out in the cold all day, why go out and freeze for an extra ten minutes now? That was a mug's game. You may want to give up the ghost today, but I want to see tomorrow!

At any other time Shukhov would have stuck to the walls like everybody else. But now he strode through the crowd and even jeered at them:

"What are you frightened of, you goats? Never seen a Siberian frost? Come out and warm up under the wolves' sun! Give us a light, uncle!"

He lit his cigarette in the doorway and went out on to the steps. "The wolves' sun" – that's what they sometimes jokingly called the moon where Shukhov came from.

The moon was high up in the sky now. A little bit more – and it would be as high as it would go. The sky was pale, and greenish. There weren't many stars, but they shone brightly. The white snow gleamed, and the walls of the barracks looked white, too. The lights of the camp glowed weakly.

By another barracks there was a black crowd of men – they were coming out to line up. Also by another barracks. But it was not so much conversation you heard from the other barracks as the sound of the snow crunching under the prisoners' boots.

Five men descended the steps from the barracks, and

then another three. Shukhov was among the three and formed part of the second row of five. It wasn't so bad standing there, having had a good fill of bread and with a cigarette between your lips. It was good tobacco, the Latvian hadn't deceived him – strong and good-smelling.

Little by little other prisoners came down the steps, and there were now two or three rows of five behind Shukhov. At this stage, whoever came out was angry at the swines still hugging the walls in the corridor, refusing to budge until the last. They had to freeze for them.

None of the prisoners ever saw a watch or a clock. Much use they were, anyway! A prisoner only has to know how soon reveille will be, how much time until parade, dinner, lights out.

The evening check was at nine – or that is what was said. It never finished at nine, they were always having a second count, even a third. You never got away before ten. And reveille was at five in the morning apparently. It was no wonder that the Moldavian had dropped off before knocking-off time. If a prisoner found somewhere which was warm, he would go to sleep there immediately. They lost so much sleep during the week that on Sunday – if they weren't hustled out to work – all the barracks were full of men sleeping.

Now the prisoners were pouring down the steps – the barracks chief and the warder, the animals, were kicking them in the ass.

"So?" the men in the first rows of five shouted at them. "You thought you were being clever, did you, you swine? Trying to get cream out of shit, eh? If you'd come out before, the check would be over by now."

The whole barracks was out now. Four hundred men – eighty rows of five. They formed a sort of tail, the rows at the front in strict order, those at the back a shambles, however.

"Line up in fives there, at the back!" the barracks' chief yelled from the steps.

But the bastards wouldn't budge!

Tsesar came out of the doorway, hunched up and pretending to look sick, and behind him a couple of orderlies from one half of the barracks, a couple more from the other half and a prisoner who limped. They formed a new first row of five, so that Shukhov was now in the third row. Tsesar was sent right to the back.

The warder came out on to the steps.

"Line up in fives!" he shouted to the prisoners at the back in a loud voice.

"Line up in fives!" the barracks' chief yelled in an even louder voice.

But still the bastards wouldn't.

The barracks' chief rushed down the steps and over to the back, swearing at them and hitting out.

But he was careful whom he hit – only those he knew wouldn't retaliate.

The men at the back got into line, and the barracks' chief went back to the steps. Together with the warder he began to shout:

"One! Two! Three!"

As each row of five was called, the men shot into the barracks as fast as they could go. That was the last of the authorities for the day.

Unless, that is, they had a recount. Any shepherd could count better than these fat-mouthed dolts. A shepherd might not be able to read or write, but at least when he's driving his herd he knows whether there's a calf missing or not. And these people had been trained, much good it had done them.

The previous winter there had been no drying-room at all in the camp, and they'd had to leave their boots in the barracks all night – and sometimes the prisoners would be chased out for as many as four recounts. On those occasions, they wouldn't even bother to get dressed, but go out wrapped in blankets. But this year they'd built drying-rooms, but not enough, so each gang could only dry their felt boots two days out of three. So now recounts took place in the barracks – and the men would be driven from one half to the other.

Shukhov wasn't the first to rush back into the barracks, but he kept a sharp eye out. He ran up to Tsesar's bunk and sat down. He tore off his boots, and climbed up the bunk near the stove. From there he put his boots on the stove – first come, first served was the rule – and then returned to Tsesar's bunk. He sat there, his legs crossed under him, one eye open to see that nobody pinched Tsesar's stuff from under the head of his bunk, the other to see that his boots were not shoved out of the way at the stove.

"Hey!" he shouted, "You, you with the red hair! Do you want a boot in your face? Put yours up, but don't move anybody else's!"

The prisoners were flooding back into the barracks. Someone in Gang 20 shouted:

"Let's have your boots."

As soon as they left the barracks with the boots, the barracks was locked after them. And when they came running back:

"Comrade warder! Let us in!"

Now the warders were collecting in the staff barracks to do their bookkeeping on those boards of theirs, to see if anyone had got away, that everyone was there.

But Shukhov did not care about such things today. Here was Tsesar, diving between the bunks towards his own.

"Thank you, Ivan Denisovitch!"

Shukhov nodded, and climbed rapidly up to his own bunk, like a squirrel. He could now finish that 200 grams of bread, have another smoke, go to sleep.

Only after such a good day would Shukhov feel so cheerful – he didn't even feel particularly like sleeping.

Making his bed was a simple matter for Shukhov: take that black blanket off the mattress, lie down on the mattress (Shukhov hadn't slept in sheets since '41 it would be, when he left home; it astonished him that women went to all that trouble with sheets – just extra washing), head back on the pillow filled with wood-shavings, feet in the sleeves of his jacket, coat on top of the blanket. And thank You, God, that's another day gone!

And thank You that I'm not sleeping in the cells, but here, which is not too bad.

Shukhov lay down with his head to the window. Alyoshka, who slept in the bunk next to Shukhov – the bunks were separated by slatted boards, had his head turned the other way so as to be able to catch the light. He was reading the Gospels again.

The light was not so far from them, and it was possible to read, even to sew.

Alyoshka heard Shukhov's thanksgiving, and turned towards him.

"You see, your soul is beseeching you to pray to God, Ivan Denisovitch. Why don't you free it?"

Shukhov glanced at Alyoshka, whose eyes were glowing like two candles. He sighed.

"Well, Alyoshka, it seems to me that prayers are like those appeals we put in. Either they don't get there, or they come back marked 'Rejected'."

In front of the staff barracks there were four sealed wooden boxes, and once a month the authorities would empty them. Many appeals dropped into these boxes. The petitioners would wait and count the days: after a couple of months, or a month, the reply would come . . .

But either it didn't come, or there it would be: "Rejected".

"That's because, Ivan Denisovitch, you don't pray enough, or you pray badly, without your whole heart, that's why your prayers don't get answered. You must pray without cease! And if you have faith, and tell a mountain to move – it will move!"

Shukhov smiled and rolled himself another cigarette. He got a light from one of the Estonians.

"Come off it, Alyoshka. I've never seen mountains

move. Well, to tell the truth, I've never seen a mountain at all. And when you and all your fellow Baptists in the Caucasus prayed – did you ever get a mountain to move?"

Poor bastards: they prayed to God, and whom did they ever harm? But they got twenty-five years all the same. That's what the sentence was these days: twenty-five years, neither more nor less.

"But we didn't pray for that, Ivan Denisovitch!" Alyoshka persisted, and, with the Gospels in his hands, he moved closer to Shukhov, right up to his face. "Of all earthly and transitory things our Lord commanded that we should pray only for our daily bread. 'Give us this day our daily bread'!"

"Our bread ration, you mean?" asked Shukhov.

But Alyoshka went on, exhorting more with his eyes than with his words, and he laid his hand on Shukhov's.

"Ivan Denisovitch, you mustn't pray to receive a parcel or for an extra portion of gruel. Things which men put high value on are an abomination in the sight of the Lord. You must pray for the things of the spirit, that the Lord will drive out all wickedness from our hearts. . . ."

"Just you listen. At our church in Polomnya there was a priest . . ."

"There's no need to talk to me about your priest!" Alyoshka begged, and his brow wrinkled in pain.

"No, but just you listen." Shukhov raised himself up on one elbow. "In Polomnya, in our parish, there's no richer man than the priest. Say you were asked to put on a roof, your price for ordinary people would be thirty-five roubles a day – for the priest, it's a hundred. And he'd pay up without a mumur. And that man's paying alimony to three women in three different towns, and living with a fourth. And the bishop's completely in his power, and you should see the way he holds his greasy hand out to the bishop. And he gets rid of all the other priests, no matter how many they send him, he doesn't want to share with anyone . . ."

"Why are you talking to me about a priest? The Orthodox Church has departed from the Gospels. And they don't get sent to prison like us because they have no true faith."

Smoking, Shukhov looked on calmly at Alyoshka's agitation.

"Alyoshka," he said, and he took his hand away from Alyoshka's, and the smoke from his cigarette blew in the Baptist's face. "Understand, I'm not against God. I'm quite happy to believe in Him. But what I won't believe in is heaven and hell. Why do you take us for fools, and try to fill us up with all that rubbish about heaven and hell? That's what gets me."

And Shukhov lay back again, flicking his cigarette ash carefully between the bunk and the window so that the captain's things wouldn't get burned. He began to think his own thoughts, and no longer heard what Aloyshka was going on about.

"Anyway," he decided, "however much you pray, it's not going to take anything off your sentence. You've got to sit that out, every day from reveille to lights out."

"But you shouldn't pray about that!" Alyoshka was appalled. "Why do you want freedom? If you were free, the remnants of your faith would be overgrown with thorns! You should rejoice that you are in prison! Here you have time to think about your soul! Paul the Apostle said: 'What mean ye to weep and to break mine heart? For I am ready not to be bound only, but also to die for the name of the Lord Jesus'."*

Shukhov looked up at the ceiling without saying anything. He no longer knew whether he wanted freedom or not. At the beginning he had wanted it like nothing else, and every evening had counted how many days he'd done, and how many were left. But then he'd grown bored. And then it became clear to him that men such as he would never be allowed home, but would be forced into exile. And he no longer knew where he would be

* Acts, XXI, 13

153

better placed – here or at home. It was impossible to tell.

Being free meant only one thing to him – home.

And they'd never let him go home ...

Alyoshka was not lying, it was evident from his voice and from his eyes that he was happy to be in prison.

"You see, Alyoshka," Shukhov explained, "it's all right for you: Christ ordered you to be here, and you are here for Christ. But why am I here? Because in '41 they weren't properly prepared for the war? Is that it? But am I to blame for that?"

"It doesn't look as though there'll be a recount ..." Kilgas shouted from his bunk.

"Yes, yes!" Shukhov answered. "We ought to chalk that up – that they're not having a recount." He yawned. "Time for sleep."

And then, in the barracks which had grown peaceful and quiet, was heard the rattle of the bolt on the outside door. A couple of men who'd been taking their felt boots to the drying-room ran in from the corridor and shouted:

"Recount!"

Then the warder behind him:

"Over to the other half of the barracks!"

Some people were already asleep. They began to grumble and move about, shoving their feet in their boots (nobody ever took off his padded trousers – without them you'd freeze up under the blanket).

"Fuck them!" Shukhov exclaimed, but he wasn't too angry, because he hadn't got off to sleep yet.

Tsesar put his hand up and gave him a couple of biscuits, two lumps of sugar and a slice of sausage.

"Thank you, Tsesar Markovitch," Shukhov said, leaning over. "Now you pass that little bag up to me, and I'll put it under my pillow for safety." (Things couldn't be pinched from the top bunks as easily, and who would think of looking through Shukhov's?)

154

Tsesar passed up to Shukhov his little white bag, all tied up. Shukhov slipped it under his mattress, and waited a while until most of the others had been driven out, so that he would have as little time as possible standing in his bare feet in the corridor. But the warder snarled at him:

"Come on, you there in the corner! Outside!"

Shukhov jumped gingerly to the floor in his bare feet (his felt boots and foot-cloths were in a good position on the stove, and it would be a shame to disturb them!). The number of pairs of slippers he had sewn together – but always for other people, never for himself. But he was used to this sort of carry-on, and it wouldn't last long.

And they'd take those slippers off you as well, if they found them with you during the day.

The gangs who had taken their boots to the drying-room – it wasn't all that bad for them either. Some of them had slippers or foot-cloths, or they went out in bare feet.

"Come on, come on!" the warder yelled.

"Do you want a bit of persuading, you bastards!" The barracks' chief was there as well.

They were all turned out into the other half of the barracks, the last of them having to stand in the corridor. Shukhov stood there, against the wall near the latrine. The floor was slightly wet under his feet, and there was an icy draught coming through the doorway.

When they were all out, the warder and the barracks' chief had another look round to see that nobody was hiding or asleep in some dark corner. If they didn't get the right number, there'd be trouble, and they'd have to recount – and perhaps more trouble, and another recount. They did their rounds and returned to the doorway.

"One! Two! Three! Four!" It was going fast now, as they were counting off one at a time. Shukhov squeezed himself in eighteenth. Then he ran back to his bunk, put his leg up on the ledge – a heave, and he was up!

Good. Feet back into the sleeves of his jacket. Blanket on top. Coat on top of that. Sleep. Now the other half of the barracks would have to come through to their side, but his lot wouldn't mind about that.

Tsesar returned. Shukhov handed him down the little bag.

Alyoshka came back. He was a bungler, he was as pleasant as could be to everyone, but he never got anything out of it.

"Here, Alyoshka!" And Shukhov gave him one of his biscuits.

Alyoshka smiled.

"Thank you! But what about yourself – you don't have anything?"

"Eat."

Shukhov didn't have anything much, but he could earn.

And now he'd have a bit of that sausage! Into the mouth! Get your teeth into it! Your teeth! Oh, the taste of meat! And the juice from the meat, the real thing! And down to the stomach!

There – gone!

He'd eat the rest of the stuff, Shukhov decided, before parade.

And he hid his head in the thin, unwashed blanket, and didn't hear the noise of the prisoners from the other half of the barracks around the bunks. They were still waiting to be counted.

Shukhov went off to sleep, and he was completely content. Fate had been kind to him in many ways that day: he hadn't been put in the cells, the gang had not been sent to the Socialist Community Centre, he'd fiddled himself an extra bowl of porridge for dinner, the gang-leader had fixed a good percentage, he'd been happy building that wall, he'd slipped through the search with that bit of blade, he'd earned himself something from Tsesar in the evening, he'd bought his tobacco.

And he hadn't fallen ill – had overcome his feelings of illness in the morning.

The day had gone by without a single cloud – almost a happy day.

There were three thousand six hundred and fifty-three days like that in his sentence, from reveille to lights out.

The three extra days were because of the leap years . . .

A Selection of History and Archaeology Titles from Sphere

INTRODUCTION TO THE GREEK WORLD (Illus.)   Peter Arnott   75p
INTRODUCTION TO THE ROMAN WORLD (Illus.)   Peter Arnott   75p
THE TOMB OF TUTANKHAMUN (Illus.)   Howard Carter   £1·50p
A SHORT HISTORY OF THE RUSSIAN
REVOLUTION   Joel Carmichael   40p
MARIA THERESA   Edward Crankshaw   75p
THE FALL OF THE HOUSE OF HABSBURG   Edward Crankshaw   50p
DAWN OF THE GODS (Illus.)   Jacquetta Hawkes   £1·00p
TUTANKHAMUN – THE LAST JOURNEY (Illus.)
   William MacQuitty   75p
SEA LIFE IN NELSON'S TIME (Illus.)   John Masefield   £1·25p
A PLACE IN THE COUNTRY (Illus.)   Barry Turner   £1·50p

History of England Series

FROM CASTLEREAGH TO GLADSTONE   Derek Beales   50p
ROMAN BRITAIN AND EARLY ENGLAND   P. Hunter Blair   40p
FROM ALFRED TO HENRY III   Christopher Brooke   40p
THE LATER MIDDLE AGES   G. Holmes   50p
MODERN BRITAIN 1885–1955   Henry Pelling   37½p

The Sphere Military Library

A HISTORY OF THE REGIMENTS AND UNIFORMS
OF THE BRITISH ARMY (Illus.) R. M. Barnes   £1·25p
THE UNIFORMS AND HISTORY OF THE
SCOTTISH REGIMENTS (Illus.) R. M. Barnes   £1·25p
MILITARY UNIFORMS OF BRITAIN AND
THE EMPIRE (Illus.) R. M. Barnes   £1·25p
WEAPONS OF THE BRITISH SOLDIER (Illus.) H. C. B. Rogers   75p
TANKS IN BATTLE (Illus.) H. C. B. Rogers   75p
THE CRIMEAN WAR R. V. ffrench Blake   60p
THE ROYAL MARINES J. F. Moulton   45p
HITLER AS A MILITARY COMMANDER John Strawson   60p

A Selection of Biography from Sphere

QUEEN ALEXANDRA (Illus.) Georgina Battiscombe	75p
MARY, QUEEN OF SCOTS (Illus.) Marjorie Bowen	£1·25p
QUEEN OF THE HEADHUNTERS Sylvia Brooke	35p
THE YOUNG CHURCHILL (Illus.) Randolph Churchill	40p
MARLBOROUGH – HIS LIFE AND TIMES (4 vols. boxed) (Illus.) Winston S. Churchill	£3·00p
MY LIFE Isadora Duncan	25p
LADY CAROLINE LAMB Elizabeth Jenkins	40p
KHRUSHCHEV REMEMBERS (Illus.)	95p
THE ROYAL HOUSE OF SCOTLAND Eric Linklater	60p
THE SUN KING (Illus.) Nancy Mitford	£1·00p
NELSON Carola Oman	75p
THE EDWARDIANS (Illus.) J. B. Priestley	£1·95p
THE PRINCE OF PLEASURE J. B. Priestley	£1·50p
ELIZABETH I, QUEEN OF ENGLAND Neville Williams	£1·00p